by
Mike Gibb

This book is dedicated to Daisy Michie

A great friend for much of my life and the inspiration for the story "The Big Hoose", although her life didn't end quite so fortuitously.

Drumorty Revisited

BY THE SAME WRITER

Books

It's A Dawgs Life
Waiting For the Master
Ask Anna (An A to Z Guide For Dogs)
How To Train Your Owner
Anna's Adventures in Wonderland
When Angus Met Donny
Where's Sammy?
The Name's Sammy, Sammy the Tammy

Musical Plays

A Land Fit For Heroes
Mother of All the Peoples
Five Pound & Twa Bairns
Sunday Mornings On Dundee Law
Clarinda
Outlander the Musical
Red Harlaw
Aberdeen's Forgotten Diva
As Long As But A Hundred of Us

Plays

Children Of The Sea
Lest We Forget
Doorways In Drumorty
Giacomo & Glover

Foreword

Lorna Moon is one of the most amazing women that the North East of Scotland ever produced and yet sadly is known by so few. Coming from Strichen in Aberdeenshire, she bore, and abandoned, three children including Richard DeMille, fathered by William DeMille and brought up as the adopted son of Hollywood director Cecil B. DeMille.

For years Lorna was the highest paid female scriptwriter in Hollywood, writing screen plays for movies starring the likes of Norma Shearer, Gloria Swanson and Lon Chaney. During her all too brief life (she died of TB when she was only 44) she also wrote two books, a novel titled "Dark Star" and a book of short stories set in the fictional Drumorty ("Doorways in Drumorty"), a thinly disguised Strichen. To say that the residents of that town were not best pleased, identifying themselves among the book's characters despite a change of names, is putting it mildly and the book was banned in the town of her birth for fifty years.

I first came across the work of the writer following the publication of "The Collected Works of Lorna Moon" in 2002 and I was instantly enchanted, so much so that I wrote a play set around a number of the book's short stories. The play "Doorways in Drumorty" enjoyed highly successful Scottish tours in 2010 and 2011 courtesy of RedRag Theatre Company and Edinburgh based theatre producer Awkward Stranger are again touring the country with the play in April/ May 2019.

This renewed interest in my play encouraged me to revisit a shelved project, a follow up book to "Doorways in Drumorty", returning to and expanding the wonderful tale of Miss Jessie MacLean and Bella Tocher and the baby. While all the other eight stories in this volume are original creations of mine they do allow the reader to renew the acquaintance of Drumorty's chief gossip, Mistress MacKenty, the dreadful farmer Skilly along with a host of newly created residents of the town.

While I am not sufficiently immodest to suggest that my writing could possibly emulate the brilliance of the wordsmith who first introduced us to the people of Drumorty, I can but hope that you will find this opportunity to revisit Drumorty rewarding.

Mike Gibb.

Drumorty 1931

I doubt if many of you have been in Drumorty for you see, it's not a terribly accessible place. To get there you take the B7912 from Auchnagatt, head for the Back Of Beyond and just hope you come across the one small faded signpost. But that said I am sure you will all have been somewhere that looks rather like Drumorty for there are hundreds of similar small, sleepy places doted round Scotland. One long main street, a handful of shops, a hotel and, of course, a church. Places that many people would class as villages but which are regarded by the residents as small towns. Refer to Drumorty as a "village" when you are there and you may be lucky to get out alive.

I jest, of course, as Drumorty is a friendly place. Well, as friendly as most claustrophobic small towns are. Now at this stage, as I am to be your window on Drumorty life, I should introduce myself. I am Jessie Maclean. Miss Maclean. Spinster. And I'll act as your narrator or one of them anyway. Mistress MacKenty was rather insistent that she should share that task.

I should think so. Just because she was a teacher and has read a lot of books she thinks she's best equipped to tell you aboot the folk in Drumorty. Nonsense. I ken mair aboot a'body's business

7

than onybody else in the hale of the place. I should. Finding oot aboot them has been my life's work. I dinna think Miss Maclean was affa happy when I telt her that I wanted to share this task but it's difficult to ken with her. I mean, are spinster's ever happy?

Anyway as I was saying, I'm Miss MacLean. Born and brought up in Drumorty. My father ran the gentleman's hairdressers when we had one but sadly the business and my lovely Dad are both long gone. I had always wanted to teach and was fortunate enough to find a post at Drumorty Primary School when I was twenty one and that is where I remained, eventually reaching the dizzy heights of head mistress, until my life changed several years ago and I opted for early retirement.

If all she's goin' to dae is spik aboot hersel' then you'll hae to rely on me to tell you a bit aboot Drumorty. There's nae an affa lot tae it nowadays as we've only the six shops. A grocer, a baker, a newsagent, a butcher, an ironmongers and, maist importantly of all, a drapers. Now it's nae just because I run the drapers that I say it's the maist important.

No, no. You see if we didnae hae a drapers then far would a'body go to get the lace for their curtains? And if they didnae hae lace curtains, how would the majority of the weemin' in Drumorty manage to watch the comings and goings withoot being seen? Thanks to my supply of lace, Drumorty is able to boast dizens of weemin' with an almost encyclopaedic knowledge of each ither's affairs.

As my co-narrator mentioned, Drumorty has its ain parish kirk, the centre point of the toun, a citadel, far gossip can be githered and exchanged on a regular basis. That kirk's been important to me for it is within its stern granite walls that I've had my ain personal trilogy. A hatch, a match and a dispatch. I was christened there when I was only twa month auld and less than twenty year later stood there looking radiant – my Ma's description, nae mine – as I tied the knot with William MacKenty. Stood there in the sight of God and, even mair importantly, in the sight of several very envious local quines who had set their cap at my Billy. Sadly twa decades later I was standing all by mysel', staring at a very funcy walnut coffin (the very best that Billy's Co-operative beerial money could buy) as he was laid to rest, leaving me a widow at....at a relatively young age.

Although I never married, there was once a man in my life. Jamie McLeod. As handsome a young man as the town ever turned out. Jamie and I were at school together, sat at adjoining desks in fact, although he left earlier than I did to serve his time with Jock Wallace, the builder. At nineteen I became his fiancé. Oh we never actually got round to getting a ring or announcing it or anything; Jamie said that he wanted to keep it as our little secret. But I knew, and that was all that really mattered. And then one day – it was the tenth of October in fact – Jamie told me that circumstances dictated that he had to go to Aberdeen so that he could find a better job and provide a higher standard of living for us.

If I can maybe just interrupt for a minute here. I should warn you that with her reading all those funcy books and having been a school teacher for so lang, that you've sometimes to read a'tween the lines of fit Miss Maclean says. So I would like to offer my services as a translator. Can we start with 'circumstances dictated' which actually means 'took cauld feet' and 'had to go to Aberdeen' which could better be described as 'ran as fast as his stumpy wee legs would cairry him'. Right, on you go.

I did think of following Jamie but it wasn't the done thing as young girls, even those engaged, unofficially, didn't run away after men. I mean, they had their reputation to think of and so I stayed behind and waited and waited. The letters, which had been so regular for the first few weeks, slowly began to be less frequent before eventually ceasing altogether.

That must be close on forty years ago and yet I can still visualise him. The thick black wavy hair, the enigmatic smile. I think that is why I became so fascinated by Bella Tocher's young man. You see, the first time I saw him, I thought, just for a split second, that it was Jamie, that he had come back at last. Of course it wasn't. Bella's lad looked barely twenty and Jamie would have been an old man by then.

But just for a second.

Drumorty Revisited

The Twinnies

Miss Agnes Sangster had a tough life of it when she was young. While other girls were out courting the local lads, Agnes was stuck at home caring for her ill, and ill tempered, Father who was virtually bedridden. No one in Drumorty knew exactly what ailed Mister Sangster although most were of the opinion that it was a severe, and apparently untreatable, case of "lazyitis".

By the time he eventually succumbed to a real illness and was laid to rest in Drumorty Cemetery, Agnes Sangster was rapidly heading towards the milestone of her thirtieth birthday and acutely aware of the fact that most of the eligible bachelors in Drumorty were now married men. Most, but fortunately for Agnes, not all and less than a year after she had a stood in Drumorty Church as a grieving daughter, she returned as the blushing bride of Sandy Robertson, a gentle lad who worked in the local feed mill.

But if Agnes Robertson thought that life's trials were behind her she was sadly mistaken. With nature's clock ticking away the newlyweds wasted no time in planning a family and within months of their wedding (a little too soon for some of the more devious minded in our midst), Mistress Robertson was delighted to proclaim to the world that she was to be a Mother. Less than a month later, clearly distraught, she announced that she wasn't. And that sadly was only the beginning of her tribulations, as time after time the poor lassie suffered a series of miscarriages.

There are few women who do not yearn to be a mother at some stage in their life and with each false dawn, that craving grew stronger within Agnes. Night after night she would sit silently in the "nursery", a room set aside for the long awaited and desperately desired baby. A room brightly decorated and filled with dolls.

But Agnes in her blighted life had one piece of good fortune. Sandy. Dear Sandy who did all in his power to help his wife overcome the void in her life by taking her for shopping trips to E. & M.'s in Aberdeen, weekends away to the seaside and, having saved up for months, on one memorable occasion whisking her off to London.

Slowly Agnes began to accept her fate and thank the Good Lord for the gift of a good husband. But in truth, the Almighty wasn't finished with her yet as three days after she turned thirty nine a miracle occurred. The arrival of a baby girl. And, as if to make up for all that lost time, a second baby appeared a mere five minutes later.

With having had the best part of a decade to decide on names, it was hardly surprising that Sandy and Agnes were well prepared in that department. If it was a boy it was to be Alexander, after his Dad; a girl was to be Doris, named in honour of Agnes's own Mother. What they weren't ready for were twin girls.

And that was when Sandy rather panicked. Agnes, clearly exhausted, wasn't in a fit state to start thinking about names and Sandy didn't want to go and tell all those waiting to hear about this long awaited and momentous event, which most of the population of Drumorty greeted with genuine delight, that his wife had given birth to "Doris and anither een". And so, responding to the first enquiry as to the babies names, he merely managed to stutter, "It's Doris and eh, eh Dor....Dorothy" and from that moment, the names were set in stone. If Agnes had subsequently expressed concern about a lack of invention, it was rather too late to do anything about it. In any event she was so thrilled by their arrival that she honestly couldn't have cared what they were called.

Besides, Agnes had other concerns to take up her mind. She had knitted the basic essentials for the baby's first few weeks using white wool, confident that she could produce apparel of a slightly larger size in the appropriate pink or blue wool as required in the fullness of time. But the appearance of twins meant that time was not a commodity she was overly blessed with. Several well meaning local mothers offered to pass on baby ware no longer required but Agnes, declining as politely as possible, was having none of it. She wasn't willing to have one of her girls in pristine new outfits and the other in "hand-me-doons".

Fortunately her sister Betty, who was equally delighted by the new arrivals, came to the rescue, knitting night and day to kit out the wee ones. It is said that Billy, her husband, who was a rather droll sort of lad, suggested that she sit well away from the grate in case the lightning movement of her knitting needles set fire to the kindling.

Doris and Dorothy were as alike as two peas in a pod, and Agnes was determined that they would be dressed accordingly. From the day they first took to the streets of Drumorty in a special pram, sent all the way from Aberdeen, they were clothed from head to foot in identical garments and from that day forth Sandy could relax about his lack of invention in the naming department as everyone who ever saw them couldn't tell which one was Doris and which one was Dorothy. And so to everyone in Drumorty they simply became known as the Twinnies.

The Twinnies had naturally enrolled at Drumorty School on the same day and left in the same orderly manner many years later. Sadly there was no employer in Drumorty who could offer a position to both of them but fortunately the Clydesdale Bank at number 46 High Street and the Watson Milling Company at 52 High Street were concurrently on the lookout for office juniors and Doris dutifully took up the post at the bank and Dorothy at the Milling Company. Or possibly it was the other way round.

Day after day, year after year, the Twinnies tripped along the High Street towards their respective places of work dressed the same. Mind you, that phrase "dressed the same" doesn't quite do it justice. For not only would they wearing identical skirts, twin sets (naturally), stockings and shoes and, no doubt the same undergarments, they also wore the same string of pearls and the same brooch and carried the same handbag over the same arm. And they walked in an identical manner so close together that they could have been mistaken for Siamese twins.

Most of the young girls in Drumorty would travel to Peterhead and Fraserburgh when they were in need of new clothes, the selection at Mistress MacKenty's shop being somewhat...limited. But even that was of no use to the Twinnies as generally speaking these emporiums would only stock a single garment in a particular size and so, visits to Aberdeen became the order of the day.

Every weekday morning they would set off from the family home in Station Road, turn the corner onto High Street, and clip clop along in their identical high heels until they reached the Bank. One would enter, leaving a second Twinnie to complete the journey to the other office, all of twenty yards, quite alone.

The Milling Company expected somewhat more for their money than the Bank, staff reporting for work at 8.30 am and not clocking off until 5 pm, but the manager of the Clydesdale was amenable to Doris's suggestion (or perhaps it was Dorothy who came up with the scheme) that his newest recruit start work early and finish late. And so their evening journey home was completed in tandem.

Despite their somewhat eccentric obsession with matched dressing, the Twinnies were relatively attractive girls and enjoyed the attention of several of the town's young men. Unfortunately, the Twinnies refusal to go out with any beau without being accompanied by her sister somewhat cooled the ardour of the male admirers and slowly, side by side, they slipped into spinsterhood, remaining at home with their ageing but doting parents.

In their early forties the Twinnies were not only united in appearance but also in grief as in the course of one tragic year they lost both their devoted Mother and Father; but, of course, they still had each other and they took over the large, if somewhat threadbare, arm chairs that sat either side of the fireplace and occupied these, evening after evening, like a pair of wally dogs. And so the years slipped by until the aged but remarkably sprightly Auntie Betty held a joint sixtieth birthday celebration in the Queens Hotel in their honour.

By then the two office juniors had risen to senior status within their respective organisations and retirement beckoned. The Watson Milling Company were extremely reticent to let Dorothy (or possibly Doris) go as she had become the lynch pin of the Drumorty office and Miss Rachel Watson, their Chairwoman, pleaded with her in a desperate if ill fated attempt to get her to stay on. Her sister was retiring so there was simply no way that she could carry on working.

As a result, on the same Friday in September, three doors apart, ceremonies were held and hominines paid to elderly ladies in dark blue wool suits who subsequently left their places of work at sharp five with boxed clocks tucked under their right arms and walked home together.

Unfortunately there had clearly been a lack of liaison between the respective employers as the Bank presented their devoted employee with an oak cased mantle clock and the Milling Company theirs with a gold carriage clock. The Twinnies had apparently planned to display the clocks on either end of the mantelpiece but when they saw that they were ill matched the clocks were confined to the spare bedroom. Both of them.

Although they were lost to the business community of Drumorty, the Twinnies remained an intrinsic part of the life of the town. Every morning, excepting Sundays when the shops were closed, they could be seen walking slowly along the High

19

Street to Browns, the newsagents, to collect two copies of the P. & J., one each, before heading along to the bakers for two freshly baked rowies. And, of course, every Sunday they were to be seen in their usual place, side by side in their pew in Drumorty Church.

It was in that very establishment that Doris took such a fit of coughing that Dorothy had to take her home before the last hymn. When her condition hadn't improved two weeks later, Doctor Thom was called and a mixture prescribed that sadly had no effect. The word began to spread round Drumorty that one of the Twinnies was "nae at all weel" with many and varied ailments being credited for her decline. One of those suggestions, pneumonia, not only proved to be accurate but fatal.

Over the years we have all seen many a grieving widow or widower and have witnessed sorrow in its many forms. But I doubt anyone has ever been confronted with a more desperate sight than that of the black clad forlorn figure, shrouded in sadness, that made her way along the High Street to the office of Mister Haggerty, Drumorty's own funeral director, the day after Doris passed away, and, arrangements having been made, shuffled back to her empty home. Several of the local women called at the Twinnies house later that day to pay their respects but got no answer to a door that they discovered, to their surprise and consternation, was locked.

The following morning Auntie Betty visited the house and found Dorothy sitting peacefully in her armchair. Peaceful and stone cold. Doctor Thom was summoned and he in turn called in P.C. Mitchell who spent a fruitless half an hour searching the house for a letter or an empty box of pills. Doctor Thom could do no more than write the words "natural causes" in the death certificate.

When Mister Haggerty heard the news he didn't know whether to laugh or cry. On one hand it wasn't often that he got two funerals in the same week; on the other, with both Twinnies gone who was going to pick up the bill? But he had no reason for concern as Auntie Betty, although not exactly wealthy, was "comfortably aff" and she was determined that her two dear nieces would have a proper send off.

But there was a problem. Dorothy had chosen an oaken casket with silver mountings for her sister but the undertaker had only one of its like in his modest establishment and spent some time endeavouring to convince Betty that the mahogany box with the gold mountings or the teak one with brass handles were just as impressive. Eventually Betty, clearly frustrated, uttered words designed to strike terror into Mister Haggerty's heart. Sinclair and Ross. For Sinclair and Ross were a well established Fraserburgh firm of funeral directors who for the previous decade had been slowly but relentlessly expanding their operation the length and breadth of Aberdeenshire. Indeed there was a rumour circulating at that time that they were looking for property in Drumorty.

Mr Haggerty had been blessed with pallor and a peeky complexion that was eminently suitable for his chosen profession and what little colour there was in his face instantly drained away when Aunt Betty mentioned those names. He knew he was beaten and he quickly assured the lady that he would drive to Aberdeen that very day and would not return without a new coffin. A new oaken casket with silver mountings.

Two days later a somewhat strange sight confronted the mourners as they trooped into Drumorty Church. In front of the pulpit, where many a coffin had stood over the years, two identical caskets sat side by side, each topped with a single matching wreath, a simple circle of white flowers with a delicate design of pink carnations in the shape of a letter "D".

But the coffins didn't just sit side by side; they sat cheek by jowl, the silver handles on the right side of one touching the silver handles on the left side of the other one.

The Twinnies were about to embark on their final journey.

Together.

Drumorty 1931

Bella Tocher. Now that was a scandal. A real twenty two carat gold een. Sadly we dinna get mony that good in Drumorty so we've really got to mak' the best of them when they come alang. When it all happened Bella was only aboot sixteen and worked up at Skilly's ferm, employed as scullery maid but daen' all the odd jobs that the auld skinflint didnae want to dae himsel'. Even at that early age Bella had naethin' in her heid but lads and it was nae surprise to ony of us that things turned oot like they did.

The first time that I saw Bella and the young man together was on a warm Sunday in June. I had decided to take a walk up round the burn before going home for my dinner as after all I wasn't in any great hurry. There was no one waiting for me other than Archie, my cat, and he was a rather contrary and ungrateful beast. I first caught a glimpse of the couple as I was coming out of the copse of trees. I know that I should have walked on but something stopped me in my tracks and it was more than just the lad's likeness to Jamie. I think that I saw something of myself in Bella. Oh, she was bonnier than I ever was, even when I was young, and yet, there was just something that caused me to stand and stare.

Whatever the reason, I hid in the woods, anxious not to disturb them, but close enough to hear all the nonsense that passes as conversation when you are courting. When I eventually headed home I was lost in my reverie, so much so that I had no appetite and gave the two dumplings to Archie, who, in his usual contemptuous manner, sniffed, arched his back and walked away. Normally I would have given him a piece of my mind. But not that day.

When the next Sunday came around, I made a rather surprising and bold decision. I wouldn't go to Church but instead would go up by the burn to see if I could see them again. Now I knew that my absence amongst the Sunday worshippers would cause some consternation but in truth, I didn't care.

Now you probably think that there are ten commandments. No, nae in Drumorty onywiy. Alongside the better kent eens like nae stealing or committing adultery there comes Drumorty's very ain eleventh commandment "thou shalt not sit in someone else's seat in the kirk on a Sunday morning". You see, we all have oor ain place in the kirk and may the good Lord hae mercy on onybody who dares to sit in it. That might sound a little petty but it's nae. It's a failsafe way of finding oot if there are ony strangers in oor midst and just as importantly, instantly showing up onybody that hasnae turned up withoot a valid excuse. Like being ill. Aye seriously ill. Nae just a caul' or flu. They dinna coont.

To give the Church a miss one Sunday could be described as brave while two in a row could be regarded as foolhardy. But I really didn't care. I needed to go back and see Bella and her young man just one more time.

I just couldnae for the life of me understand why Miss Maclean wisnae at the kirk. Again! Somebody said that she had a sair throat but you surely dinna miss the kirk for that, certainly nae twa wiks in a row. So after a few of us had discussed the matter at some length, it was agreed that somebody would hae to go roon to her hoose and discover just fit was goin' on. I volunteered.

When she came to the door she had a scarf wrapped aroon her throat and she said that was the reason that she hadnae been at the kirk. I telt her right oot that I couldnae accept that and I pointed oot that earlier that day she had been spotted walking up towards the burn. You'll never believe what she said. 'I went out for a breath of fresh air to see if it would help my throat'. Did she tak' me for a feel? Fa had iver heard of fresh air bein' good for you fan you were ill? Onywiy I telt her straicht that she better be in her place on the following Sunday or else the new minister would think that she didnae like his sermons or feel they were o'er lang. Which they were. That fair broucht her to her senses.

I was horrified by the thought that the new minister might conclude that my absence was something to do with him as nothing could be further from the truth. I took a great deal from his sermons and unlike many of my fellow parishioners, didn't find them overly long. I therefore decided that there would be no more spying on the young couple and that coming Sunday I would be in my regular seat. After all, the new minister had had a difficult enough introduction to Drumorty life without me adding to his woes.

You see his arrival was greeted with very mixed feelings as the Church divided into two factions. On one hand we had the selection committee that had chosen him and who made it clear that they were delighted with their choice. The other smaller, but considerably more vociferous group, comprised of those who were not invited to be part of the selection committee but thought that they should have been and who consequently wrote off the man before he had even uttered the first syllable of his first sermon. I was a member of neither grouping and tried to ignore the many and varied criticisms of the man.

A'right, I accept that I wisnae happy with him back then. Still nae delighted with him the day to be honest. But back then he was affa..... affa ....

What Mistress MacKenty would really like to say at this point is "new". You see that is a complaint that has been levelled against every incumbent of the post since the Church was built. New ministers are apparently to be distrusted on the basis of their newness, right until a month before they are due to retire at which point they are showered with accolades.

I wisnae goin' to say new. I was goin' to say that he was affa young.

True. But as I rather suspected, he did grow out of it.

And he was an incomer.

I don't believe we've had a minister that was born in Drumorty.

I ken. But at least the last een came frae Aiberdeenshire.

Yes. But Macduff isn't that far away.

But it's in Banffshire! And besides, he's affa religious.

I had always thought that would be a benefit but not apparently amongst the majority of the congregation in Drumorty who seemed to equate being religious with long sermons and long sermons with being late in getting home for their Sunday lunch.

But amongst all the many and varied criticism levied at the Reverend Stephen there was one with which I had to agree. He was single and badly needed a wife alongside him to help navigate the choppy waters of Drumorty life. Fortunately there was not a shortage of woman folk in the town willing to help him overcome that particular problem and there, right at the front of the queue, was Mistress Forbes.

When she was younger Peggy Forbes was full of fun, larger than life in fact, but sadly the years took their toll. Or rather her one woman crusade to try to find a husband for her only daughter Mildred did. That wasn't an easy task. The problem was Mildred was...plain

Plain! Fit dae you mean plain? If you're goin' to come up with rubbish like that, then it would be better if I telt this story. Mildred was ....dreepy. That's all there is aboot it.

I'm sorry if that sounds a bit uncharitable but you have to be honest in these situations. Back then, Mistress Forbes had already spent years trying to get Mildred hitched, failing miserably. Now lesser weemin' would hae thrown in the towel. But nae Peggy Forbes. She kent that if she couldnae get Mildred mairried aff, then she would never get to be a Grunnie.

The New Minister

A Grunnie. It wisnae much to ask for was it? One wee grandchild to sit on her knee. Somebody to tak' for a walk roon the toun on a fine Summer's day or to sit and knit cardigans and mitts and booties for in the lang winter nichts. She kent it wisnae going to be easy to find a man for Mildred. I've heard folk say that if there was a beauty contest in Drumorty and Mildred was the only contestant, she still wouldnae win. So Peggy started her search early, a'fore Mildred turned eichteen in fact, and she thoucht that if she was goin' to dae it then she had better dae it properly.

So she got a notebook and wrote doon the names of all the eligible men in the toun. A book with twa columns, een for positive attributes, een for negatives. When she had completed an entry she would add up the plusses and then deduct the minuses and the een with the best score would be her first port of call. Originally, the only men that got intae the book were those that were good looking, that had a job with reasonable prospects and a hoose of their ain. But o'er the years as one by one the lads were snapped up Peggy got less choosy and by the time Mildred was thirty they got intae the book if they were single and had a pulse.

That was why the arrival of a new minister, a single man, was like Manna from heaven and Peggy immediately snapped intae action, inviting him for lunch on the very first Sunday he was here. That was afore onybody else could dae it as she kent that it could very well be Mildred's last chunce of finding a man and her last chunce of becoming a Grunnie.

"*Mildred, gie your hair a raid up. How would the new Minister want to mairry onybody looking like that?*"

"*Fa said I wanted to mairry him onywiy?*"

"*Why would you nae? He's seems like a nice young chap.*"

"*I'm nae sure I want to be a Minister's wife.*"

"*Mildred, you've been turned doon by ivery ither profession known to mankind. A Minister's all that's left. Please try. For my sake.*"

"*Aye, a'right.*"

"*Good girl. Now fan he comes to the door, you answer it. Tell him that lunch is nae quite ready and ask him if he funcies a stroll roon the gairden with you.*"

"*But Ma, there's a gale force win' blawin'.*"

"*Dinna exaggerate. Onywiy, you're a bit too sturdy to blaw awa'.*"

"*Ma!*"

"*That'll be him now. On you go. And if he tries to haud your han', just you let him.*"

"*No!*"

"*I'm only talking aboot huddin' your han'.*"

"*But fit will the neighbours say?*"

"*They winna see you for the hedge. Now on you go.*"

"*I'm goin'. I'm goin'.*"

To no one's surprise he didnae try to haud Mildred's han'. Still at least Mildred didnae manage to scare him awa', as she had daen with some ithers, and she certainly didnae put him aff his food. Peggy telt me that she didnae ken fan the lad had last sat doon tae a proper meal, probably during the Boer War by the looks of it, but he couldnae half eat. Twa plates of tattie broth. Roast chicken with skirlie and all the trimmings. And twa helpings of Jam Roly Poly. So it was nae a great surprise that he jumped at the chunce of returning the next Sunday.

A Minister is always regarded as a catch. Nae because of the money but because of the prestige. And so it was nae a shock that Peggy suddenly found that she had competition from quite a few Drumorty Mothers with unmarried lassies on their han's.

But she had at least the advantage of being in first and she was determined nae to gie up withoot a fight. And so it became a regular feature of Drumorty life, watching a tall thin form entering the Forbes hoose every Sunday about one o' clock only to emerge twa hours later looking considerably less emaciated. Everybody commented on the fact that the number of hens pecking around the Forbes back gairden began to reduce and folk got used to the sight of Peggy returning from the butchers every Seturday, laden doon with parcels.

O'er the course of twa month the Minister became a regular Sunday visitor and started to feel like een of the faimily. He even suggested that while he was in the hoose that they no longer refer to him as Reverend but could in fact call him Mister Stephen instead. That's a bittie overly familiar to my mind but if that was what he wanted then fa was Peggy to argue?

Unfortunately, his idea of being a member of the Forbes faimily meant that he treated Mildred as a sister and naethin' mair. Every Sunday for eicht wiks, in all weathers, him and Mildred would trump roon and roon the gairden, flattening the grass in the process, but niver once did he try and tak' her han'.

Peggy found hersel' in a bit of a quandary. With the amount he ate, he was costing her a sma' fortune. But should she give up and waste all money that she had already invested or keep going for a while langer in the hope that he would eventually fall in with her plans? She decided to gie it another fower wiks and nae a day mair. As it turned oot, however, things resolved themselves lang afore then

"Ma, Ma!"

"Fit's the matter Mildred?

"Ma, it's the Minister."

"Did he mak' advances towards you?

"No!"

"Oh. That's a peety. So fit's wrang?"

"Ma. He's attached."

"Attached? To fit."

"It's nae a fit. It's a fa."

"Just fit are you haverin' aboot lassie?

"He's attached to a quine. Een that bides in Macduff. Ma, he's got a.....fancy!"

"A fit?"

"A fancy. He's engaged."

"You mean a fiancé."

"Aye, een of them."

"How dae you ken?"

"Because he telt me. Said he wouldnae be able to come for his dinner next Sunday because he was going to MacDuff to see about the plans for the wadding."

"He'll mean a wadding far he's conducting the ceremony."

"That's exactly fit I thoucht for a start. So I asked him 'Oh fa's getting mairried?' And fan he said 'me and my fancy' you could hae knocked me doon with a feather."

"It would hae to be fairly big feather."

"Ma!

"Sorry. That's terrible news."

"I ken. I mean he could hae said something."

"How could he? He's mooth has aye been stuffed with food. Food that I boucht with your Da's hard earned money. He's had four chickens, twa pound of best steak, liver, kidneys, a couple of dabs of lemon sole and I dinna ken fit else. And that's withoot mentioning the soups and the puddings."

"Double helpings."

"Aye, double helpings richt enough."

"That's stealing Ma."

"You ken this Mildred, you're right. Takin' food under false pretences is stealing. Well, if that's the kind of man that he is then you're better aff withoot him. I think this has been a lucky escape."

"Really?"

"Aye really. Now, far's the book?"

"Oh no Ma, nae the book."

"Aye the book. First of all we'll hae to tear oot the pages aboot that thief. And then we'll hae to start a new entry."

"A new entry?"

"Aye. A brand new entry."

"But fa?"

"Remember that Mistress MacKenty drapped in past the ither day? Well, she was the bearer of good news."

"Mistress MacKenty broucht good news? That must be a first."

"Richt enough."

"*So fit was this good news?*"

"*You ken Charlie Henderson that ferms up at Hillside?*"

"*Aye, I ken him. He's married to Elsie.*"

"*Nae ony mair. That's the good news. Elsie's deed! We've got a new single man in the area.*"

"*Ma, Charlie Henderson's aboot sixty.*"

"*Rubbish! I found oot that he's only fifty eicht.*"

"*Oh Ma!*"

"*A'ight. We'll put doon his age as the first entry in the minus column but we'll balance it up because of the fact that he's got his ain hoose, his ain ferm and, from what I'm telt, his ain teeth.*"

"*Ma, I'm nae in the humour for daen this the day.*"

"*You're richt, you've had a trying day. We'll dae it in the morning.*"

"*Thanks. But Ma is Charlie Henderson nae just aboot blind?*

"*Aye he is that. Right. I'll put that doon as a plus.*"

"*Ma!*"

Drumorty 1931

Peggy's knitting needles are still gathering dust as sadly, despite all her best endeavours, she was never able to find a man for Mildred. Some lassies are apparently destined to be spinsters and that's all there is about it.

I never thought that Bella Tocher would have that problem as during that winter of 1925 her courtship with the young man seemed to flourish. From time to time I would go up past the burn after the Church on a Sunday. I didn't eavesdrop you understand; I always stood far enough away so that I couldn't hear what they said to each other. No, it was just the delight of watching them together, so comfortable in each other's company that I enjoyed.

It so reminded me of Jamie and I all those years ago. In fact at times it almost felt that I was watching my early life being re-run, as if it had been captured on one of those new fangled movie machines. For you see, up by the burn had always been our favourite spot, the place where we would meet. Oh, we certainly weren't alone in that; many young couples courted there. But to me it was always our special place and I think Jamie might have felt the same way.

It was early in the spring that the first warning signs appeared.

Sunday after Sunday I saw Bella standing at the end of the road that led to Skilly's farm, looking in vain for her young man. Then one week she was nowhere to be seen and it became clear that the romance was over.

It may not have been a major scandal at that stage but it certainly kept a section of Drumorty's female population in gossip for several weeks, speculating on what had happened to him. Various theories buzzed around the town – he'd gone to join the Army, he'd run away with someone from the visiting fair, he's gone in search of work. Of course no one knew for sure so they just made up stories. As usual.

The picture did become clearer, however, when Bella began to.....bloom. That was when Drumorty had a real scandal on its hands and a meeting of the Church elders was called to discuss what to do about the "shameless hussy".

.

The Holiday

I first encountered Jennifer Cooper when she arrived as a sweet little five year old and I knew instantly that she was special. Most children of that age come to Drumorty Primary school tightly clutching their Mum's hand and trying desperately to hold back the tide of tears we all knew would come the very moment that their Mother started to leave. Occasionally, however, one would arrive with a remarkable level of self-assurance for one of such tender years.

Jennifer fell into neither category. She was happy to be at the school, anxious to listen and to learn, but yet always delighted when her Mother collected her at the end of the school day. And that attitude never altered. Indeed, I remember meeting her many years after she left school, on the day she started work in the Doctor's surgery, and thinking how little she had changed. Oh her hair was no longer tied up in bunches but the deep dark brown eyes still shone and she had retained the ready smile that could brighten the darkest day. There and then I knew that Jennifer Cooper would have a lot of love to give and so it proved.

Unlike most of her contemporaries in Drumorty, she was in no hurry for a band of gold on her finger. She enjoyed the company of many of the local lads but never had a steady boyfriend, more than happy to flit from one to the other, leaving many a forlorn boy in her wake. She was equally content in her work as receptionist to Doctor Thom, offering a friendly and reassuring greeting to those visiting the surgery. Then, in the course of a few short months, just before she came of age, she went from being Jennifer Cooper, femme fatale to Miss Cooper, spinster.

She was an only child that stayed with her Mother and Father in an old granite cottage at the west end of the High Street. Her Mother was a poor soul, nervous and, in her mind anyway, permanently in ill health. Mind you it wouldn't have been easy staying with Raymond Cooper.

Mister Cooper was a handsome man. It was just a pity that he knew it. As a result he particularly enjoyed talking to ladies, especially the young attractive ones, and he possessed the gift of the gab essential for his work as a salesman with the Liverpool Victoria Assurance Company,

He was also somewhat short on discretion and it became positively embarrassing that Mistress Cooper seemed to be the only person in Drumorty that didn't realise that her husband was....ehm, befriending Miss Grant, the postmistress.

It came to a head one day in November when it was discovered that the post office hadn't opened for business. When we heard that Mister Cooper had been seen leaving the town early that morning, people began to speculate on what could have happened. They came up with several answers as I understand it, before eventually concluding that Mister Cooper and Miss Grant had run away together.

When I heard, I was speechless; probably the only person in Drumorty that was, and when it became clear that it wasn't just a minor infatuation and that they weren't coming back, Mistress Cooper took to her bed and refused to eat. She never rose again and three months later they buried her.

At the funeral Jennifer cut a lonely, solitary figure, alone in her grief, alone in the world with all efforts to contact her father having met with failure. Diverse rumours on his whereabouts circulated around the town and while none could be confirmed, it seemed clear that Mister Cooper was gone for good. Jennifer's relatives were somewhat thin on the ground, the nearest, in terms of both relationship and geographical location being her late mother's sister Auntie Kathleen in Inverurie and although invited, she had no wish to leave Drumorty and her job to go to live there.

The manner in which her Father had betrayed her put her off men and it looked that, like me, she would end up an old maid, living with just her cat for company. But as it turned out, both of us were wrong about our long term prospects.

With a well paid job in the Doctor's surgery and having lived so long with her parents, Jennifer had been able to accumulate quite a substantial nest egg with apparently nothing to spend it on. Except that Jennifer had plans.

Very few people in Drumorty went on holiday. Mistress Nicholson had a relative in Blackpool she sometimes visited in the summer and Mistress MacKenty and her husband had the occasional long weekend in New Pistligo but that was about it. Certainly no one had ever heard of anyone from Drumorty going abroad.

It therefore created quite a bit of a stir, and a lot of gossip, when Jennifer announced that she was going on holiday for ten days. To Venice. In Italy! After she returned, looking as brown as a berry, she was invited by the Women's Guild to give a talk on her adventures and she was happy to oblige, bringing along lots of photographs of St. Mark's Square and the Bridge of Sighs and the many other wondrous sights of that magical city. She also told a hushed audience of how she got there by sleeper train and boat and day train through a host of countries we only knew of from looking at an atlas. It was a most enjoyable and informative evening.

It was many months later before we realised that Jennifer had been a little economic with her description of her holiday adventures, holding back facts about some of her exploits and choosing not to make us party to all of the photographs that had been taken. Eventually however the truth came out.

She had spent the first few days in Venice in the traditional manner of all tourists, riding on a gondola and visiting St Mark's Cathedral and the many other ancient religious buildings. She even dug deep into her holiday spending fund when she discovered that there was a Puccini festival on and spent a magical evening in La Fenice watching the death of Mimi.

The first couple of nights she ate in the main tourist traps but found the food indifferent, the service offhand and the prices excessive. On the third night, however, she stumbled across a small family restaurant in a back street and seated herself in one of the handful of outdoor tables. Everything about the experience was perfect including the waiter, a rather attractive gentleman who identified himself as Antonio.

The following evening she made a charade of checking the menus of a couple of neighbouring restaurants although she had already decided where she would eat. Antonio graciously welcomed her and at the end of the evening brought a glass of a brown liquid, which he explained was made from almonds and was "on the 'ouse".

At first Jennifer was a little uncomfortable eating on her own while every other table boasted couples, some becoming more and more amorous as the evening wore on and the wine count increased. On the second evening there, however, she didn't in fact eat alone as she suddenly became aware that a pair of eyes were focused on her, belonging to one of the many stray dogs roaming the streets of Venice searching for food.

Although this particular creature was very skinny, with his ribs showing beneath a wiry and dirty coat, there was a spark of life, a spark of independence in those shiny eyes that she admired and she began to feed him pieces of bread and scraps of meat. Antonio was all for shooing him away but she wouldn't let him. She was happy to have a dinner companion.

By the time of her third visit, the restaurant owner and Antonio were both waiting to show her to "her table" while her four legged friend turned up within minutes of her being seated. The evening concluded with two complimentary glasses of Amaretto.

On the Saturday night when Antonio announced that the restaurant was closed on Sundays her heart sank a little. He explained that on his day off he would be heading back to his home village and eating in a little restaurant there. Perhaps she would like to accompany him so he could show her a little of the countryside?

Even as he was still speaking into one ear, Jennifer could hear the voice of sanity whispering in the other *"Are you mad?"Are you really thinking of going in a car with a stranger who is probably only after one thing? Well, two if you include your money."*

As a stoic Scot she knew that there was only one sensible answer. *"No thank you."* But just as she was about to say that, an image came into her mind of a skinny, downtrodden stray dog with a spark of life and independence that had no doubt lived more and had more adventures in a few years than she had had in all her life. And suddenly a voice, which sounded remarkably like hers, said *"Yes Antonio, I would love to go with you."*

He collected her from her hotel the next day in a car he had managed to borrow and which, with a lot of work, could have been described as beat up and they headed away from the hustle and bustle of Venice to the peace of the countryside. The restaurant proved to be little more than a room in an elderly lady's home in a charming village of white washed houses and the dish of the day was just that. The bill, which they split, was embarrassingly small even including the bottle of wine which they shared.

The wine loosened her tongue and she told Antonio about her life, every boring detail which he listened to intently, apparently fascinated by tales of Drumorty life. He in turn revealed his desire to get away from the Veneto region of Italy, where he had lived everyday of his life. His vision was to travel and told her that he had *"always dreamed of seeing Scotland"* although Jennifer doubted that he had even heard of it before meeting her. When he dropped her back at her hotel she thanked him for a memorable day. What she didn't add was that it had been the most memorable day of her life.

Then all too soon the last few days of her dream holiday slipped by. On her last morning Antonio visited her at hotel, as she had suggested, and joined her by the pool, his bronzed physique turning a few head and setting many tongues wagging including that of a dreadful woman called Wilma who hailed from Horsham in Kent. Within ten minutes of meeting her Jennifer had made a mental note never to visit Kent.

All too soon it was time for a farewell and tears ran down Jennifer's face as she watched Antonio walk away. She knew it was destined to be no more than a holiday romance but yet.... And then, before she knew it, she was staring out of the window of a train ploughing through the Mearns countryside beneath leaden skies.

But she really wasn't too aware of where she was or what she was seeing as her mind was totally pre-occupied by the mad cap scheme she had come up with as the train was crossing France.

Could she possibly implement it?

Her Aunt was waiting for her at the Joint Station in Aberdeen and over a pot of tea in the nearby Station Hotel Jennifer told Aunt Kathleen exactly what she had in mind. Not surprisingly, her Aunt was horrified.

"Has the sun frazzled your brain?"

While she wouldn't admit it to Kathleen, when she analysed it in the cold light of an Aberdeen day she harboured serious doubts about the wisdom of the plan that she had first flirted with in the warmth of the Italian sun. But she had to give it a try. She owed it to herself. And if truth be told she owed it to the poor women of Drumorty; after all this could prove the best bit of gossip since an elder was found selling some of Communion silverware at Milne's Auction House.

"I know you think I'm crazy."

"Yes I do. But I understand. Things look so different when you are on holiday."

"I agree."

"You know so little about him."

"True."

"You'll end up paying the travel costs to get him over here. And no

doubt lots of other expenses."

"I know."

Jennifer did know that every sensible word that Kathleen said was right. But she went ahead regardless, ignoring the advice of not only Kathleen but several friends who had been alerted to her plans by her well meaning, if rather interfering, Aunt.

Kathleen had been correct on one front. Jennifer was forced to dip heavily into her savings as the costs proved more than she had ever imagined. But as they snuggled together on the sofa in her wee Drumorty cottage, oblivious to the sleet battering on the windows, she knew that every penny she had spent had been worth it.

She sneaked a sly glance at her companion. At the muscular torso and the shiny black hair and the deep brown eyes and her heart fluttered. Yes, definitely worth every penny.

On becoming aware of her attention, Glen pushed his muzzle further across her knee and settled back into a contented sleep, years of begging for scraps in the back streets of Venice, and even the six months spent in quarantine kennels, long forgotten.

Jennifer hadn't gone to Venice looking for love. But she had found it.

Drumorty 1931

An emergency meeting of the Church Elders was duly convened and I didn't have long to wait for news of the outcome, enjoying a visit bright and early the next morning.

"Good morning, Mistress MacKenty. And to what do I owe the honour of a visit, especially at such an early hour."

"I'm here to tell you aboot the meeting of the kirk elders last nicht."

"Oh yes."

"They reached a decision. A unanimous decision."

"About what?"

"Aboot fit should be daen with Bella Tocher."

"I didn't realise that Bella was a Church member."

"She nae. We wouldnae hae her."

"So why would the elders be discussing her?"

"Because of the shame she's broucht to Drumorty."

"Shame?"

49

"*For goodness sake, far have you been these last few months? Surely you've heard aboot her meeting some young lad every wik. And on the Sabbath!*"

"*Yes.*"

"*And now he's awa' and left her. And left her in a … condition.*"

"*Yes I knew all that. But I still don't know what that's got to do with the Church.*"

"*Because it's oor duty to uphold the morals in this toun. See that its nae broucht into disrepute by shameless hussies like her.*"

"*She's just a young lassie when all is said and done. So what have the elders decided?*"

"*They decided…unanimously mind!*"

"*Yes you said.*"

"*They decided that Skilly should sack her forthwith and that she be telt to leave the toun withoot delay.*"

"*But where will she go?*"

"*That's hardly oor concern.*"

"*You can't put her out on the streets. Not in her condition.*

"*She should hae thoucht of the consequences afore she got hersel'* into that condition. Onywiy the decision has been made and that's all there is aboot it. Skilly will ensure that she's aff his property by twelve o' clock the morn's morning. And that's why I'm here."

"I'm not sure I understand."

"We assume that she will be takin' the train to Aiberdein. The first een the morn is at twelve thirty and she'll nae doobt catch it. Now to get from Skilly's ferm to the station she'll need to wa'k the length of the High Street."

"I assume she will."

"Well we've decided to gie her a send aff she winna forget in a hurry. So we want abody that has a window that faces the High Street to be lookin' out at the back of twelve. And at the moment that she passes, you are required to pull doon your blinds."

"But why?"

"To send a message to her that she is nae wanted here. Just in case she should ever think of coming back."

"I greatly doubt she would think of doing that."

"We're better to mak' sure. You never ken with that kind. Richt, so you ken fit to dae?

"Oh yes I know well enough."

"Good. I'm awa' to see Mistress McWilliam next door now."

I decided to stay one step ahead of the rest of the town by pulling down my window blinds there and then and sat in the darkness, lost in memories. Memories of when I had been the lass left behind. Oh because I wasn't in Bella's condition the good and compassionate people of Drumorty let me stay although I was suitably chastised for my foolishness in "carrying on" with a young man. I sat and cast my mind back to that time all those years ago and wondered; if I had that moment to live all over again what would I do? In my heart of hearts I think I knew.

But there were other more pressing issues to consider and I admit I spent a sleepless night, wrestling with my conscience. I woke early and was amazed when I looked out at eight of clock and found that there was a palpable air of excitement in Drumorty as groups had gathered on doorsteps to discuss the great event that lay ahead. It was mildly reminiscent of the Coliseum with the Romans waiting for the Christians to come and pet the Lions. And yet by twelve o'clock all was suddenly hushed and still the length of the street. Nothing stirred with the exception of the merest flutter of a lace curtain.

And then Bella appeared.

The Concert

There aren't many people in Drumorty that someone doesn't say a bad word about. In fact I can think of only one; Robert Forrest the joiner. For Robert is as kind and as amiable a man as you are ever likely to encounter and a fine tradesman as well who discharges his duties with great professionalism. The only criticism anyone could ever level at him, if it is a criticism, is that Robert can be rather dilatory in sending out his bills especially if he is aware that the customer is undergoing temporary financial embarrassment.

Aye Robert Forrest is a'right. Except for that horrible smelly pipe that he aye smokes and his taste in music. I should explain that there's nae much to dae on a winter's nicht in Drumorty. To be honest there's nae muckle to dae on a summer's nicht either but at least then you can hae a walk alang the High Street as far as the Brig, hae a look at the burn and then walk back.

So everyone was delighted when they started having concerts in the Beaton Hall. Initially these were very well attended until the clientele found that there was in truth a somewhat limited repertoire of artists willing to travel to Drumorty to entertain with the result that the same acts would appear on a very regular basis. Into that category fell the GG Trio from Rothienorman who could be seen in the hall every month and on occasions even more frequently.

I think I should tell you a bit about the GG Trio. For a start there are three of them although you have probably already worked that oot for yoursel'. And their name has naethin' to dae with horses but comes from the leader of the group, Gladys Gardiner, a great lump of a dame who disnae so much sit on the piano stool as engulf it and who, with fingers like Fowlie's best sassiges, batters the piano keys into submission. Gladys is accompanied by Sidney Meldrum on the accordion, a decent player but a cheerless sort of lad who aye looks as if he has just been telt that smiling has been rationed. And the trio is completed by Harry Gove, a grand fiddler whose fingers seem to dance across the strings.

Because of their very regular appearances, the audiences to see the GG Trio dwindled and dwindled until most times there was little more than a handful of folk shivering inside the cavernous and barely heated hall. But you could guarantee that amongst them would be Robert Forrest, entranced by Harry Gove's brilliance on the fiddle, and accompanied as always by Andy.

The last time I went alang, there were fourteen folk in the hall and that included Jimmy Sangster, the hall keeper, and his wife Bunty, who was only there to provide the half time sandwiches. I went alang because Mistress McIntosh telt me that she had heard that Mistress Ramsey had a new lad, only six month aifter she had beeried her man, and that it was rumoured that they were baith going to the concert. Turned oot to be a total waste of time as they niver turned up. Fa was there, of course, was Robert Forrest.

Robert is a devoted family man. A year after Mary and him were married, Sheila came along followed by another daughter, Emily, two year later. While Robert doted on both girls he longed for a boy and when Mary fell pregnant again he was beside himself, telling everyone who would listen that he was going to have a son and that he was going to be called Andrew, after his own father. And then Mary gave birth to a lovely, healthy baby.... girl. It is said that Robert was devastated for all of thirty seconds until he held her in his arms and looked down into her bright blue eyes and then he was smitten.

Because he was so convinced that it was going to be a boy, he refused to even consider choosing a girl's name and so Andrew became Andrea. In many ways Robert got his wish as Andrea, or Andy as she insisted on being called from the time she was three, was an out and out tomboy with no interest in dolls or scraps or any of the things that so enthralled her sisters. I still remember Mary telling me that the little madam refused to wear the bonnie frocks and shoes handed down by her sisters, insisting on wearing dungarees and wellies.

Andy and Robert became inseparable and it was no great surprise when she regularly accompanied her Father to the town hall concerts which was just as well as her Mother had made it clear that she wouldn't sit through another evening in the company of the GG Trio *"for all the money in the Ellon Branch of the British Linen Bank"*. But Robert's side of the family had always been musical. I can still remember popping into a neighbour's house one Hogmanay – for a small sweet sherry, nothing more – and being entertained by Robert's father who after a dram or two was always willing to bring out his mandolin, his speciality being a Stephen Foster medley of "Old Folks At Home" and "Oh Susanna" and his party piece, "I Dream of Jeannie With The Light Brown Hair".

When I eventually left the Hall (perhaps escaped would be a better description) at the end of that lang nicht, I watched Robert Forrest, his pipe already polluting the nicht air, deep in conversation with his daughter. It was only later that Mary revealed that although that was the sixteenth or seventeenth time he had seen the GG Trio, that was the nicht that Robert reached a momentous decision and came home grinnin' like a Cheshire cat.

"You're looking affa pleased with yoursel' Robert. Are you sure you've been to the concert in the hall?"

Drumorty Revisited

"*Aye Mary.*"

"*And how was it? The same as last time? And the time afore?*"

"*Nae exactly. They played a couple of new tunes.*"

"*Really?*"

"*Well there was definitely one new tune. The other might just hae been Gladys and Harry playing aff of different music sheets. But there is a reason for me looking so pleased with maesel' as you put it.*"

"*Oh aye and fit's that?*"

"*On my way hame I reached an important decision. I've decided to give up smoking my pipe.*"

"*Niver!*"

"*Now dinna you try and spik me oot of it Mary. My mind is made up.*"

"*For goodness sake, why would I want to dae that? I've been trying to get you to get rid of that affa thing for the last twenty year.*"

"*I niver really understood why you felt so strongly aboot it.*"

"*It might hae something to dae with the fact that it stinks up the hoose. And that you have hardly ony jumpers or cardigans than dinna look as if they have been attacked by a band of sterving moths."*

"Onywiy, you can put awa' your darning wool for good."

"But why have you decided this aifter all these years?"

"Because I need the money that I spend on tobacco. You see I am saving up for something."

"Fit?"

"I canna tell you. It's a surprise."

"And fan will I find oot."

"Oh it'll be a while yet. I reckon I will hae to save up my allowance for quite a few months. So you'll just hae to be patient."

True to his word Robert gave up buying tobacco and although for the first week he looked like a cat on a hot tin roof, he stuck to his vow and religiously, week after week, deposited the money saved by his sacrifice in a jug. It took something like four or five months for it to accumulate to the desired level but eventually he was convinced that he had sufficient and early one Saturday morning Andy and him set off in the van to Turriff. Even after stopping off for a sandwich, they were home by three o'clock.

Visits to Turriff were a fairly regular event for the Forrest family, Robert always managing to time them to coincide with a Junior game at The Haughs while Mary headed straight for the elegant department store on Main Street. On a previous visit Mary had mentioned to Robert that she had seen a large oval mirror, explaining that it *"would look right bonnie above the mantelpiece"*.

Why Mary thoucht for a minute that such information had lodged in her man's heid, which at the time was clogged with memories of the fitba match a'tween Turra and Banks O' Dee he had just been to watch, only she could explain. But with their silver wedding coming up, she added two and two the gither and came up with an answer of eight pound ten shillings, the exact price of a certain oval mirror.

Mary was standing on the doorstep as they arrived home, clearly delighted to see them, and with an air of expectation as Robert removed a parcel wrapped in brown paper from the back of the van.

"Did you twa hae a successful day?"

"Oh we certainly did."

"And did you get fit you went to Turriff for?"

"Indeed. Exactly fit I wanted to get. Look."

"It's nae affa bonny wrapped."

"Fit dae you expect fa a pawn shop?"

"A Pawn shop? So fit is it that you boucht?"

"This."

"A fiddle! You canna play the fiddle."

"I ken. But I'm goin' to learn. Someday I hope to be able to play like Harry Gove."

"So that's why you've been goin' to all these concerts in the Hall."

"Aye."

"At least that explains something. For a while I thoucht you were gettin' a bit saft in the heid. But fit mak's you think you will be able to learn the fiddle. I mean you tried your Da's mandolin and couldnae mak' onything of it."

"The mandolin has an affa lot of strings. This looks easier."

"We'll see. But I canna believe that you went and spent all the money you've been saving for months and months on that."

"*Nae all the money. I boucht something else.*"

"*Really?*"

"*Aye I boucht this as weel.*"

"*You spent good money on that!*"

"*It's a music stand.*"

'*I ken it's a music stand. And a right rusty auld een at that. Fa ever selt you that must hae seen you comin'.*"

"*The mannie that rins the pawn shop gave me a special price since I was buying twa things.*"

"*If you paid mair than ten shillings total, you were robbed. But why would you need a music stand.*"

"*To pit sheet music on.*"

"*But you dinna hae ony sheet music.*"

"*I ken but I can buy it anither time.*"

"*You canna read music.*"

"*True. But I can learn and meantime I thoucht it might look classy in the corner of the good room. With books or something on it.*"

"How could a lump of rusty metal possibly look 'classy'? Oh Robert, I give up. Onywiy, come on then. Since you spent all that money on this fiddle let's be hearing you."

"I canna play tunes or onything yet."

"I realise that."

"But the mannie in the shop showed me the scales."

According to Mary she listened as long as she could. But when the cat started howling and ran out of the room, she accepted that enough was enough.

"Stop it. I canna stand it ony langer."

"But Mary I'll hae to practice."

"Then dae it somewhere else."

"Far?"

"Go into the good room."

"I thoucht we werenae supposed to go in there unless the Minister or somebody else important was visiting."

"Aye, but I'll make an exception in this case."

"Are you sure you'll be happy if I practice in the good room?"

"Robert, judging by your efforts to date I would be happiest if you practiced in your brither's hoose in Auchnagatt. But as I doobt he would welcome you, on you go. And tak' that rusty thing with you."

The fiddle played by anyone who is less than proficient is not an attractive sound and even through two doors and two walls the sounds emanating from the good room night after night were driving Mary mad. And so, accompanied by the other family members (excepting Andy who provided moral support to her Father) Mary would leave the house as soon as the "music" began and walk around the town until she was sure that it was safe to go back home.

Then one night as Mary and the two girls returned to the house they were more than slightly surprised to conclude that they could actually detect a tune. It wasn't exactly wonderful but it certainly was a lot less unpleasant than the din they had been subject to up until then. In an effort to encourage him, Mary told her husband of her thoughts when he emerged.

"Robert that sounded....nae bad."

"Thank you."

"In fact we wondered if you might want to come through into the kitchen and gie us all a tune?"

"*No, I dinna think so.*"

"*You've nae need to be shy.*"

"*It's nae that but you'll just hae to wait and piy your money the same as a'body else.*"

"*Fit are you talking aboot?*"

"*The Annual talent concert in the Beaton Hall next month.*"

"*Oh Robert, you hinna?*"

"*Aye.* "

"*Do you ken fit you are daen?*"

"*You said that it sounded good.*"

"*No I said it was 'nae bad'. There is a difference.*"

"*Oh well, perhaps some extra practice is needed a'tween now and three wiks on Seturday.*"

The Annual talent contest normally attracts the same people, year in, year oot. Folk playing the spoons or singing auld bothy ballads, occasionally in tune. Or Geordie Walker, the local Slater, daen his ventriloquist act with his dummy, Jockie, made from timmer left o'er when Geordie was helping to pit up a new byre reef at ein of the ferms. For a slater he made a good job of fashioning the dummy; it was just a peety that he niver mastered the art of keeping his ain mooth closed when the dummy was supposed to be speakin'.

So the fact that there was to be a new act on the stage that year increased the interest in the contest and ticket sales were brisk.

By the time that I arrived at the hall, it was well filled. Right at the front sat Mary Forrest with a spare seat alongside, reserved by a strategically placed coat. There was no sign of either Sheila or Emily, both having totally refused to attend and suffer the embarrassment of watching their Father make a fool of himself in front of half of the population of the town, while Andy was obviously backstage with her Dad giving him encouragement.

The first half followed the usual pattern with the same old faces and even in the case of Jocky, the same old jokes, leading to the tea interval which involved a stramash as folks tried to get hold of at least one of Bunty's famous scones. Then the tea things were cleared away and Billy Thomson, MC for the night, appeared in front of the curtain and announced that we should *"give a big Drumorty welcome to someone who is new to the stage of the Beaton Hall"*. Out of the corner of my eye I saw a shadow of a figure slip from the wings into the Hall and, moving the coat, sit down in the seat beside Mary Forrest.

It was Robert Forrest.

"Robert! Robert fit are you daen here? Oh love, I'm so sorry."

"Dinna be."

At that moment the lilting sound of "I Dream of Jeannie With The Light Brown Hair", played sweetly on a solo fiddle, filled the hall and the curtains opened to reveal the slight but confident figure of Miss Andrea Forrest.

"Andy, its Andy. But how? Have you twa been learning the fiddle the gither?"

"Naw lass, it took me less than a wik to appreciate that I was hopeless. These muckle hands were never meant to play onything delicate. But Andy, she's a natural."

Not another word was spoken by the couple as they sat, hand in hand, letting the lovely music wash over them. And then as the last note died away, Robert was on his feet clapping and cheering. And before long he was joined by every person in that place, realising that they had, for the first time, witnessed real talent on the stage of the Hall.

Looking at the beaming face of Robert Forrest, with tears running down his cheeks, it became clear that he would have been proud to have stood on that stage and played the fiddle but not half as proud as he was watching his Andy up there.

Drumorty 1931

Bella was dressed in a shabby coat that had most certainly seen better days and clasped a brown paper parcel, all her worldly possessions, to her chest. She looked relieved to find that she wasn't being confronted by any of the righteous residents of Drumorty and was heading in the direction of the Station when "woosh", the blinds on Mistress Paterson's front window were pulled down with real venom. The lassie stopped in her tracks but after taking stock of the situation hurried on. Then "woosh" a second blind descended. Then a third.

By this stage Bella's head had dropped and her slow walk had developed into a hurried scuttle. When a fourth blind fell I could take it no longer and went out of the house and after her.

"Bella".

My initial call was ignored so I tried again.

"Bella".

She stopped and looked round.

"Oh so you've come oot intae the street so you can gloat up close have you Miss Maclean?"

"No lass."

"So fit dae you want?"

"I'd like to help you."

"Me? That's broucht shame to Drumorty."

"Not in my eyes you haven't. Please let me help you."

"But why?"

"Because once, many, many years ago, I was like you. Oh I wasn't expecting a baby or anything like that but I was lonely and scared and I know that back then I would have done anything for a kindly word."

I could see that she was caught on the horns of a dilemma. Should she head out of the town that had brought her so much pain or should she trust me in the hope that I might, just might, be offering her the shoulder to cry on that she desperately wanted and needed?

I decided to try just the once more.

"Come on into the house and I'll show you the wee jacket. The one I'm knitting for the baby."

"My baby?"

"It's hardly likely to be mine is it? And I'll put the kettle on."

"But fit's the point. If I miss this train I'll just hae to catch the afternane een instead."

"You don't need to catch any train if you don't want to. I've got a spare bedroom."

"You mean, stay with you?

"Yes."

"Me and...the baby."

"Of course."

"But fit will folk say?

"Bella my dear, it's a long time since I cared what folk said about me. A very long time."

And as I took her little bundle from her and led her into the house, I knew that people would undoubtedly speak about me. But I also knew that, truthfully, I couldn't care less.

Drumorty Revisited

.

The Medals

Shirley Davidson was born in Drumorty. As were her Mother and her Father and both sets of her Grandparents. Shirley was died in the wool Drumorty and had never had any ambition to leave, even for a day out in Fraserburgh or Aberdeen. She was contented with her lot.

While others had pipe dreams of owning a fur coat or getting a run in one of those new motor cars or taking the train all the way to Edinburgh to see the sites, Shirley wanted nothing beyond what she already had. A tidy, if small, house on Park Road, a hard working husband (Danny Davidson was the local blacksmith) and a son Gavin who was the light of her life.

From an early age Gavin showed no great desire to play football with the other boys or to go and swim in the White Loch in the summer days, preferring to sit in his bedroom and read. Read anything and everything he could get his hands on although his particular favourites were the works of Charles Dickens and he read them all, over and over again. In fact it became a tradition for him to read "A Christmas Carol", cover to cover, on the 24th of December each and every year.

As a consequence of his studious nature he became the star pupil at Drumorty School and was destined to become the first person from the town, ever, to go to Aberdeen University. He secured a place which he could take up as soon as he turned eighteen, and until he reached that milestone worked as a clerk in the law offices of Stephens and Hall. He proved to be such an asset that both Gregory Stephens and Gerald Hall asked him to consider returning to their office after he had completed his University studies, sanguine that he would sail through his Law degree.

Gavin celebrated his eighteenth birthday on June 15th, 1914, and thirteen days later Archduke something or another was shot in a city with an unpronounceable name in a far off country. The lights went out all over Europe. Including Drumorty.

Danny Davidson was a decent and upright man who had a great belief in King and Country and when the call went out for men to join the Gordon Highlands, he immediately answered it. Gavin was left in a quandary; should he follow his dream of going to the University or follow his Father? To no one's surprise he chose the latter.

Initially Shirley was caught up in all the excitement especially when the lads got their uniforms and they both looked so handsome. The beautiful blue and green kilt, a sporran twice the size of the tabby from next door, all topped off with a Glengarry worn at a jaunty angle. She was so proud of them both and tried hard to keep the seed of worry that nagged away at the back of her mind at bay; after all, everyone said it would all be over by

Christmas.

Shirley was one of a large group of Drumorty residents who had gathered at the railway station to watch the men head off to the front line. Although there were only five men from Drumorty joining up at that time, they were given a proper send off with the High Street draped with bunting and the Ellon and District Pipe Band marching with them as far as the Station.

Shirley stood on the platform, a wee Union flag in one hand and a hankie in the other, and waved and waved until the train was out of sight, the billowing smoke in the distant sky the only evidence it had ever existed. While she was at the Station, surrounded by most of the population of the town, including a lot of rather sheepish looking young men, she was bursting with pride. By the time she made the short walk back to Park Road and her empty abode, however, pride had been replaced by a veil of desolate sadness.

Being an only child Gavin and his father had always been close but living and fighting alongside each other, day after wretched day, meant that the bond grew and strengthened. They helped each other to cope with life in the trenches; the cold and the mud and the rats and the mind numbing boredom of the days when nothing happened.

That closeness also diminished their individual fear of being

injured or killed as they worried more about the safety of each
other and it was that attitude that ultimately saved Gavin's life.

By November 1916 their battalion was stationed in Ancre in
France and were part of a big push against the German 1st Army.
On the second day of the battle the whistle sounded and the men
of the Gordon Highlanders scrambled out of their trenches and
headed towards the German lines. Gavin was half a step behind
his father who suddenly saw an enemy shell exploding in front
of them and in a split second had the presence of mind to push
Gavin back into the trench. Gavin survived; his Father didn't.

Over the course of the first two years of the war Shirley enjoyed
a stream of letters from the trenches, short and cheery from her
husband, lengthy and often profound from her son. She began to
believe that the war surely couldn't last much longer and that
her two precious boys would be safely returned to her.

But then the letters suddenly dried up. At first she convinced
herself that because of what was going on neither of them would
have the time to write or perhaps the mail just couldn't get
through. Convinced herself until the dreaded telegram arrived
informing her that Danny had been killed on the second day of
the battle and was buried on some foreign field.

Initially there was no news of Gavin but eventually word filtered
through that he had been wounded. Pieces of shrapnel had been

removed from his head in a field hospital before he was sent back to a military establishment somewhere in England for rest and recuperation.

It was six long months before he was officially demobbed. His war was over. Shirley waited day after day for him to walk through the door until she received a letter, the content of which she found somewhat strange, requesting that she "collect him" from Aberdeen Royal Infirmary at Woolmanhill. It was only when she arrived there she understood.

Gavin looked the same in many ways. There was a nasty scar across the side of his brow extending onto his scalp but otherwise he looked uninjured. But when she stared into her son's eyes and saw a deep empty void, she realised that the Gavin she knew, the bright young lad, was gone. Forever.

His Mother took him by the hand as they left the Infirmary, reminding Shirley of his first day at the school, and spoke to him all the way home on the train, pointing out everything that they passed. Gavin spoke not a word, not a single word.

For the first few weeks Gavin wouldn't leave the house but slowly but surely he went out shopping with his Mother although he never acknowledged anyone they met on their travels. And it broke his Mother's heart to see him shake and burst into tears when someone slammed a house door loudly or one of the few cars that ever passed through Drumorty backfired.

After a few weeks, however, Shirley accepted that if he was ever to get back to something even remotely resembling his former self that she would have to remove the shackles and allow him to go out on his own, safe in the knowledge that he would never venture far. It was around this time that the daily confab of the town's top gossips outside the post office remarked on the disappearance of the thin metal caps from the bottles of milk left on their doorsteps. For a start they blamed it on birds but it soon became clear that the tops were not being pecked but removed intact.

It was a mystery that was solved one morning as they stood chatting and were approached by Gavin Davidson who posed a question.

"Do you like my medals?"

The group of ladies stood dumfounded as they looked at Gavin's jacket which was decorated by row after row of 'medals', handmade by Gavin who had attached the silver milk bottle tops to pieces of ribbon before fixing them to his jacket with safety pins. When he got no reply, he asked again. And again.

"Do you like my medals?"

Eventaully, one of the women responded confirming that they were *"very nice".*

"I got them from the King."

With that, satisfied that he had imparted sufficient information, Gavin scurried off before stopping outside the butchers, apparently staring at the array of meat products on display. He repeated this feat outside the grocers, the bakers, the newsagents, the ironmongers and the drapers and only then did it become clear to the small watching crowd that Gavin wasn't looking at the content of the various windows. He was admiring himself, and more importantly his medals, in the reflection.

Before long the sight of Gavin with his proud chest of medals became commonplace and locals were always ready to respond to his *"Do you like my medals?"* query with a curt *"Yes they're very nice Gavin. Bet you got them from the King"* which seemed to satisfy him and send him on his way.

There is little in the way of crime in Drumorty and so there has never been a resident policeman, the local bobbie, P.C. Mitchell, staying in New Deer and looking after several towns and villages in the area. He was therefore more than a little surprised, not to mention excited, when he was summoned to Drumorty to investigate a break in.

Bill Turnbull, the owner of the Ironmongers, arrived to open his shop one morning only to discover that someone had beaten him to it although rather than using the entrance door they had gained entry by smashing their way through one of the display windows. The cash float left overnight in the till had been taken together with a selection of quality hand tools.

P.C. Mitchell was delighted at the opportunity of acting like a real policeman and strutted up and down the High Street, notebook and pencil in hand, interviewing everyone that he met, enquiring as to whether anyone had any information on any other, perhaps unreported, thefts in the area. No one had, well....except for the theft of milk bottle tops.

This information was of great interest to the policeman; after all theft was theft and the name of the culprit, Gavin Davidson, was duly noted. Over the course of that day, P.C. Mitchell was regularly informed by concerned locals who explained that Gavin spent a lot of time staring into shop windows and that, yes, several of them had seen him on numerous occasions looking into the Ironmongers. There was also the matter of Mistress Nicholson's personal ladies garments going missing from her washing line. Not that they were alleging that Gavin was responsible but after all the laddie wasn't *"right in the heid"*.

A preliminary report was duly completed and forwarded to Police headquarters in Peterhead and two days later a large black car drove along the main street in Drumorty and turned into Park

Road, stopping outside the Davidson residence. Two gentleman of the law emerged and requested the opportunity of speaking to a Mister Gavin Davidson in private.

Ever since his Army days Gavin had been in awe of men in uniform and if these men, one of whom actually had Sergeant's stripes on his arm, suggested that he had broken into the Ironmonger's shop then maybe he had although he certainly couldn't remember having done so. They also seemed interested in the content of his pockets, which he emptied onto the kitchen table at their request, especially the collection of silver coins which they told him amounted to two pounds, seven shillings and sixpence.

If his Mother had been allowed to sit in on the interview she could have explained that Gavin received a postal order from his Auntie in Dundee every birthday and every Christmas and that Gavin liked to cash them at the post office, taking the money in shiny coins which he never spent but loved to look at. But, of course, his Mother wasn't there and as Gavin had difficulty in remembering what happened that very morning, he could offer no explanation of where the money had come from.

A little more than an hour after it had arrived, the car left Drumorty with one additional occupant.

The court case didn't last long. When the Police Sergeant read out his notes about the strange behaviour of the accused, the unexplained money and most importantly the fact that Gavin hadn't denied that he had broken into the shop, there really was only one possible outcome. Gavin was sentenced to six weeks in prison.

Shirley was in court and became almost hysterical, pleading with the judge and trying to explain that there was simply no way that Gavin could spend six weeks in a prison cell.

She needn't have worried. Four days later Gavin Davidson hung himself using the sheets from his prison bed.

There were four people present at the graveside when Gavin's body was laid to rest in Drumorty Cemetery. Shirley, her sister from Dundee and two men from the funeral parlour. It wasn't that the locals didn't want to pay their last respects but rather that Shirley Davidson made it abundantly clear that no one, not even the minister, would be welcome.

Two months after Gavin was laid to rest, the Press & Journal carried a story about the arrest of a gang of men who had been breaking into large houses all around the North East. When they were apprehended, they were in possession of a large number of hand tools, several with the name Turnbull & Son, Drumorty stencilled on the wooden shaft.

Shirley's sister tried to persuade her to leave Drumorty and to go and live with her but she refused. She was determined that the people of Drumorty would have to see her daily as a constant reminder of what they had done to her son. She never answered the door to any callers but still went about her daily business as before.

Well, not quite as before. She spoke to no one other than to ask for a loaf of bread or a half pound of mince, always accompanied by the appropriate please and thank you, but nothing more and efforts to engage her in chit chat about the weather or how she was keeping were met with a stony silence.

Gradually the sad tale of Gavin Davidson began to slip into Drumorty folklore as other events captivated the minds and tongues of the locals. But if they thought that was the end of it they were gravely mistaken. For on 15 June 1917, on what would have been Gavin's twenty first birthday, a strange thing happened.

As Mister Turnbull arrived to open his shop that morning he discovered that both display windows had large posters plastered on them. Posters that contained a photograph of Gavin Davidson, looking resplendent in his pristine Gordon Highlanders uniform, with the words *"Gavin Davidson, 1896-1917, Murdered by the good folk of Drumorty"* below it.

The posters were quickly taken down by the shopkeeper

although not before several people had seen them. Those who heard about it through the Drumorty grapevine were most upset that they arrived too late to view them with their own eyes but they didn't need to be concerned. For on the same day the following year, and every other 15th of June until Shirley Davidson passed away, the exact same posters appeared on the exact same windows.

"Murdered by the good folk of Drumorty".

Is there anyone in Drumorty who could dispute that statement?

Drumorty 1931

My actions in providing shelter for Bella Tocher were viewed with a mixture of amazement and suspicion and for quite some time Bella and I were shunned when we walked down the street and given the cold shoulder in most of the local shops.

As Bella's date grew ever closer she was less able to get out and about and I was more than happy to stay home and keep her company, delighted to have someone to speak to in the long, dark winter nights.

And then as the first signs of spring emerged, Bella gave birth to a wee boy that she named Lawrence and life for both of us changed. I quickly realised that Bella had no real interest in being a mother and was more than happy to let me take on jobs like changing nappies and washing baby clothes, tasks which some women would describe as a chore but which were a joy to me. I felt like a mother to them both and revelled in a role in life that I believed would never come my way.

On top of that Miss Watson, the lady who lived in what was known by everyone in Drumorty as the "Big Hoose", paid her sewing bill of three pounds ten shillings which enabled me to buy a cradle and a pram for the wee one.

All was going really well until a knock on the door announced a visit, an unwanted one, by Stanley Anderson, the cheerless and self important Session Clerk at Drumorty Church.

"Good morning Mister Anderson. It's a bit of surprise to see you at my door."

"Oh is it?"

"Well you seem to have been rather reluctant to visit me these last few months. Since I have had a house guest in fact."

"Ah well, it is your "guest" that I've come to see."

Now I have always regarded myself as an honest person and have tried hard not to tell lies. But when confronted by a hypocrite like our esteemed Session Clerk I felt that I could make an exception.

"I'm afraid that you've had a wasted journey."

"Oh. Why?"

"Miss Tocher is out at the moment and I'm not sure when she will return."

"Could you tell me far she is?"

"I could. But I prefer not to."

"*Then perhaps you can pass on a message?*"

"*Yes I can do that.*"

"*Tell her that her situation has been discussed by the kirk session. At length.*"

"*I can certainly believe that.*"

"*And the Session concluded that if she would just face the Elders and admit her sins...*"

"*At what sins are those?*"

"*You ken only too weel and it would be quite inappropriate for me to discuss such matters with an unmarried lady. As I was saying if she will just admit her sins, then we can find a place for the bairn in the alms-hoose....*"

"*The baby already has a home.*"

"*...and that Mister Skilly is willing to tak' her back. Nae at the auld rate of course but he is willing to pey her half of what she was getting a'fore.*"

"*Oh but that's just too kind of Mister Skilly, willing to let the lassie do all the unpleasant tasks on his farm for half the price he would pay anyone else.*"

"I've delivered the message, so I'll tak' my leave of you."

"Just you do that. And Mister Anderson."

"Yes?"

"Don't hurry back."

I will admit that I was shaking a bit after I closed the door, slightly abashed at the manner in which I had addressed the man and aware that Bella, hiding in the kitchen, had heard the exchange. Not surprisingly Bella burst into the room the moment that Mister Anderson had left.

"I ken I'm nae much of a Mither to the bairn, but you wouldnae let them tak' the wee lad to the alms-hoose, would you?"

"That wee lad will be taken out of this house over my dead body."

And I meant those very words.

The Loon

Skilly was always referred to as that. While everyone else in Drumorty was spoken about and addressed as Mister or Mistress or Miss, Skilly was always just Skilly. I am sure that he has a first name but in the fifty odd years since I first came into contact with him I have never heard anyone, including the farmer himself, use it.

It has been suggested in certain circles that he deliberately uses only one name in case somewhere along the line he is charged by the letter. Now I do try not to speak ill of anyone but even I would have to admit that where money is concerned Skilly is rather mean, a man who could make Ebenezer Scrooge look like a philanthropist. He also had a reputation, one that was hard earned, of being equally mean in his manner; dour would not be an unfair description of him.

And yet he wasn't always like that as when he was young he was personable and regarded as a bit of a catch. He was eventually hooked by Barbara Thomson the baker's youngest daughter and they moved into the large and rather elegant farm house at Burnside Farm, Skilly's mother and father having vacated it in favour of a small converted cottage. The newlyweds had a rosy future to look forward to, especially after

Barbara bore him the son he craved for. Everything seemed perfect until Barbara contracted TB and didn't linger long.

Skilly changed overnight into the bad tempered hermit that most people in Drumorty came to know. He refused to send his son to school, insisting that the lad would get all the education he needed working alongside his father. The boy was christened Richard, in honour of his maternal granddad, but would always be referred to by his father as the "loon". That was when he was in a reasonably charitable humour; other times he would call him the "gype".

Burnside has always been a profitable farm, extending to over fifty acres of good farming land and with a reasonable herd of cattle, a few pigs, hens and half a dozen dairy cows. An operation that could provide ample work for a couple of experienced farm hands. Skilly insisted on running it himself with the only help coming from the loon and a constant stream of young girls who were employed as general skivvies.

Now this might have worked out not too badly if Skilly himself had been a grafter but sadly he wasn't. Oh he tackled certain aspects of farm life like feeding the animals and most folk in Drumorty reckoned he got on better with the beasts than he did with people; he certainly spoke to them more. But when it came to back breaking work he was invariably posted missing, leaving it for the loon to complete.

The farm house at Burnside boasted a plethora of rooms but Skilly vowed to save money in heating bills by occupying as few as possible. Consequently the place was so cheerless that the loon eventually chose to stay in the bleak cold quarters of the bothy, with only the mice for company, rather than have to face the morose face of his father, meeting only for meals which passed in strained silences. It wasn't much of a life but it was the only one the loon had ever known or believed he could look forward to.

The young girls that Skilly employed were generally of little help. Most were reluctant to work hard for the pittance that Skilly paid them and quickly became disillusioned by the drudgery of the life and moved on. But Bella Tocher was different for Bella was a hard worker and the loon was not only grateful for the help she provided but also enjoyed her company.

He also admitted to himself that she was quite an attractive wee lassie. He knew there was a boyfriend on the horizon but daydreamed that perhaps it was only a passing infatuation and that in the fullness of time Bella might look kindly on him.

Not surprisingly then the loon was devastated when he heard that Bella had been dismissed. Suddenly he was being stripped of his workmate, his friend and, just possibly, his sweetheart. The loon plucked up the courage to broach the subject with his father, proposing that a proper farm hand be employed to share the workload but his suggestion was dismissed out of hand and three weeks later a slip of a girl with an aversion to hard work arrived to take over Bella's duties. That was the straw that finally broke that loon's back.

Skilly came down to breakfast the next morning to be greeted with the news that the loon was gone. An inspection of the bothy revealed that all his meagre possession were nowhere to be seen and later that day his worst fears were confirmed by several eye witness accounts of the loon having been seen boarding a bus and heading out of Drumorty.

Skilly was left with a difficult decision. The girl he had employed was little better than useless and the farm wouldn't run itself. He had two choices. Work hard himself or put his hand in his pocket and actually pay a proper wage to a proper farm hand. He opted for the latter or rather he endeavoured to do so but adverts placed in the Press & Journal week after week, at not inconsiderable expense, met with no success. Clearly Skilly's reputation has gone before him and no one wanted to live their life under his shadow.

The young girl lasted less than two months and wasn't replaced, leaving Skilly quite alone, rattling around the big house and failing quite miserably to maintain the farm. Week by week the situation got worse as the tendrils of neglect ensnared all aspects of life at Burnside Farm. Indeed there were days when Skilly didn't even get out of bed until the roaring of the cattle alerted him to the fact that they hadn't been fed. Skilly overcame that particular problem by carting them all off to Maud mart.

One advantage of Skilly's thrift was that he had built up quite a substantial bank account and for the next few years he regularly dipped into that nest egg in an effort to keep afloat. But while it may have been substantial it wasn't bottomless and before he knew it he found himself sitting across a large highly polished desk from Mr Wallace, manager of the Drumorty branch of the Clydesdale Bank.

"Mister Skilly, as we have written and informed you, you are dangerously close to being penniless. Can I ask what you intend doing about it?"

Skilly shuffled about uncomfortably but said nothing.

"You may not like what I am about to suggest but in truth I think that the only way out is for you to sell the house and the farm."

There was still no response from the remarkably penitent farmer.

"Mister Skilly?"

"If you think there's naethin' else I can dae then let's go aheed. Can you handle the sale for me?"

"Of course. Be delighted to. I will set the wheels in motion right

away."

The potential sale of Burnside caused quite a stir in Drumorty with what seemed like half of the population coming along to look, the majority for no other reason than pure noseyness and perhaps the chance to smirk at the plight of the rather unpopular owner. However there were several visitors with a genuine interest in buying the place.

A genuine interest until they saw its condition, that was. The house had descended into what was little more than a ruin, with all but one room, in which Skilly lived and ate and slept, boarded up. Sadly the farm had fared no better with the roof of the byre showing signs of sagging due to nail sickness and the few farm implements that he hadn't managed to sell off, rusting away.

Not surprisingly no offers were received and Skilly's financial position worsened to the extent that he no longer opened most of the mail that he received from the Bank knowing only too well that it would merely be to advise him that yet another cheque had bounced.

Then the day came when a telegram arrived at Burnside Farm requesting the urgent attendance of Mister Skilly at the Clydesdale Bank at 11 am the following morning and he knew the game was up. He could hide no longer.

When Skilly entered the manager's office in the Bank the following day initially nothing appeared to have changed since his last visit all those months ago. Mister Wallace was wearing the same blue pin stripe suit, the same white shirt, the same paisley pattern tie. But then he realised that something was different as Mister Wallace was smiling.

"Good morning Mister Skilly. Please take a seat."

"Thank you."

"I am delighted to be the bearer of some good news. We have a buyer for Burnside Farm."

"Really?"

"Yes."

"How much?"

"The full asking price."

"Aye but does this buyer hae the siller?"

Mr Wallace gave a short laugh before replying.

"I don't think you need to worry on that score. While I am not currently in a position to reveal the name of the purchaser let's just say that he is well known in the North East, being one of the district's wealthiest gentleman.

"If he's that well aff, fit does he want with my ferm?"

"His eldest daughter has just got married and he's giving it to her and her new husband as a wedding present."

"A wadding present? Burnside Ferm? Has he seen it?"

"Not exactly but he has seen all the photographs that I took. Of course they intend carrying out major refurbishment before they move in."

"Aye, they'll need tae."

"In fact the young couple and their architect intend coming along to see it tomorrow morning provided that is convenient for you."

"Aye that's fine by me."

"Super. So I'll bid you farewell. And incidentally the cheque should be in your account by the end of this calendar month."

"That's wonderful. And eh, thanks for all your help Mister Wallace."

"You're most welcome Mr Skilly. Good day".

Skilly barely slept a wink that night, concerned that it was all too good to be true, that it was an elaborate hoax by someone that wasn't too fond of him and there was no shortage of them in Drumorty. But then at exactly 10 am the following day a large car with the Rolls Royce flying lady sitting splendidly atop the bonnet gingerly made its way along the potted road leading to the farm and three figures emerged.

A smartly dressed young man with a very attractive young lady, who immediately took his arm, followed by a distinguished dapper gentleman who Skilly assumed was the architect. The young couple approached and Skilly was still wondering if he should bow when the young man spoke.

"Sylvia, this is my father."

Skilly stood and stared. And stared until eventually he had regained sufficient composure to ask.

"Is that...is that you...loon?"

"No I'm Richard and I am proud to say that this rather beautiful young lady is my wife."

"But ...fit happened....how....?"

"Did this all come to pass? In truth I had three great pieces of good fortune. The first was gathering the courage to leave here. And you. The second was landing the job as handyman on Sylvia's father's estate. And the third, the best of all, was encountering a truly remarkable man who was willing to entrust his precious daughter to a common working laddie like me."

"So you intend biding here?"

"Yes. I have some happy memories of this place, when my Mother was alive that is. This gentleman is Mr Ferguson our architect who has organised the renovation work which is due to begin very soon."

"They are making a start on Monday, Richard."

"Nae this Monday?"

"Yes, Mister Skilly. This next Monday."

"But I hinna found onywiy else to bide yet."

"I suppose we might be able to help you there Father."

"Could you?"

"Oh I don't see why not. You are certainly welcome to stay in the bothy until we are ready to knock it down. It's a bit draughty as I remember but I'm sure you will get used to it. Right, Bernard, Sylvia shall we have a look around?"

And as Richard Skilly accompanied by his lovely wife made their way towards the ramshackle house, Skilly realised that the loon was not a loon anymore. He had grown up. And for the first time in a long time, Skilly actually smiled.

Drumorty 1931

Gradually the animosity that the locals felt towards me abated. I am not sure it was out of any feeling of fondness for me or my guests but rather that the good people of Drumorty had found some other event to occupy their days and their minds. Whatever the reason when I took the wee one out in perambulator no one bothered to cross to the other side of the street and a few even greeted me with a smile and an enquiry about the baby's health.

Those first six months of the little one's life were amongst the happiest days I could ever remember but sadly the same couldn't be said about Bella who became increasingly moody and morose, brooding over the lost boyfriend.

I still remember the morning that I entered the silent parlour and espied the letter waiting for me. In truth I hardly even needed to open it to know that Bella had gone.

I don't think I had ever felt quite so lonely and I'll admit that I collapsed into the big chair and wept. But then I heard a sound. At first I thought I was merely imagining things but as the noise grew louder it became clear that it was the sound of a baby crying.

I rushed into the other room and there he was, lying in his cot. It was then that I realised that Bella was gone and, judging by her letter, wouldn't be coming back and that the baby was mine, all mine.

As I sat and nursed him in front of the fire I thought of Bella, a poor lass who had run away in the night, run away with money that was mine, desperate to try and find a young lad who in truth probably had no wish to be found.

And I will admit that the joy I felt for my great fortune was tempered by the sadness I felt for the plight of that poor girl.

The Big Hoose

Even nearly thirty years later everyone who lived in Drumorty at the time could remember the night that Daisy arrived. Not the night itself; she apparently turned up at about three in the morning, having walked the ten miles from Peterhead in the pouring rain, but we all could remember hearing about it later as the story leaked out. Not that Daisy herself had any great desire to recollect the events.

Lots of people had spoken to Daisy long before that fateful night as she was a fairly regular visitor to the house of Mister and Mistress Kidd who lived with their son Michael in Back Row. Now in a town where every woman was addressed as Miss or Mistress, and never by their Christian name, Daisy was strangely always called just Daisy.

Her friendship with the Kidds dated back many years to when Daisy and Catherine Hunter, as she was back then, had both worked in a licensed grocers shop owned by Daisy's brother in Peterhead and although they both subsequently married, the friendship forged as young girls working in the back shop, weighing potatoes into paper bags and many other similar, and equally boring, tasks remained steadfast. For that Daisy was extremely grateful in the turbulent times that led to her midnight flight to Drumorty.

Little was ever said about Daisy's husband although Mistress Kidd, in a moment of minor indiscretion, once referred to him as a bully and a wastrel. What was known is that on that momentous night all those years ago, Daisy returned to her wee flat near the harbour, having worked late in the shop making up the next day's deliveries, to find it empty. Empty not only of all other living souls but empty of every stick of furniture, every ornament and nick-nack, every article of clothing she possessed. Three years of creating and feathering a nest wiped out in a single evening. She was left, quite literally, with the clothes she was wearing.

She sat down on the bare, hard floorboards and cried and cried until eventually she composed herself sufficiently to realise that she couldn't sleep in that empty cell. The simple solution would be to go her brother's home nearby but she couldn't cope with the shame. Nor with the 'I did warn you about him' that would undoubtedly emanate from her brother nor the smug smile of her sister-in-law with whom she had never been on terribly favourable terms.

There was only one refuge available and if that happened to be ten miles away, so be it. And so she trudged out of Peterhead, amidst the dark and the gloom, vowing never to return and was in a sad and seriously bedraggled state when, several hours later, she knocked on the door of the wee cottage in Back Row. Fortunately the warmth of the welcome provided by Cathie and Alex more than compensated for all of the hardship of the open road and almost before she had time to recover her breath, she found herself enveloped by a man's dressing gown, sitting in front of a roaring fire and sipping a very welcome cup of tea.

The make-do bed that was created for her that first night became her nightly resting place for the next few weeks but although Cathie and her husband repeatedly told her that there was no rush to do so, Daisy knew that she had to find permanent lodgings of her own and some form of employment to pay for it.

But if life had been far from kind to her, that suddenly all changed as on the first day of her search she discovered that they were looking for a live-in housekeeper at Rosebank House, the property referred to by every occupant of Drumorty as the Big Hoose. Daisy applied and was immediately hired.

When Samuel Watson left school he began working for a grain merchant in Fraserburgh and one of his many tasks was to cycle round the farms in the Drumorty area, collecting cheques from farmers who had somehow forgotten to pay their bill. Over a cup of tea and a homemade scone, the farmers would bend his ear about the trials and tribulations of farming. One of the most regular complaints that was voiced was the time wasted and cost incurred in transporting their grain to the feed mill in Fraserburgh and, if it was being milled, the cost of bringing it back as animal feed.

A seed was planted in Samuel's brain and when, on one of his many visits to Drumorty, he passed a semi derelict building with a large "For Sale" sign, that idea took root and grew. Despite the condition of the building Samuel could see that with a bit of work it would make an ideal feed mill. A visit to a local bank manager with a sympathetic ear, who was clearly impressed by the enthusiasm of the young man, secured a loan and the Watson Milling Company opened its doors.

Always aware of the right side of shilling, local farmers flocked to it, delighted to be able to save a bit of time and money and before long word spread and the Watson Milling Company began to enjoy business from further afield. Within five years Samuel was in position to repay the bank loan but having talked it over with the manager, mutual agreement was reached that the monies accumulated would be better spent on building a house for the Watson family, Samuel having gathered a wife and two daughters, Rebecca and Rachel, along the way and like always Samuel thought big and built the finest house in Drumorty. The Big Hoose.

The Watson empire continued to grow through a combination of building new mills in neighbouring towns and buying out some of the company's smaller competitors. While Rebecca took the well trodden path of marrying young to a local farmer and producing a son, Ronald, and a daughter, Amanda, Rachel's chief interest in life wasn't boys but the success of her Father's business and she began work in the Milling Company's High Street office on the Monday after she left Drumorty School.

Helping her Father to continue to build the business consumed her every waking hour and she just never had the time to find a husband or have children of her own. Not that she didn't like bairns. In fact she loved to spend time, on the odd occasion when time allowed, with her niece and nephew and was extremely generous to both on birthdays and at Christmas.

Rachel had just celebrated her thirty first birthday when her world was turned upside down. A sudden heart attack robbed the town of Drumorty of its only entrepreneur and Rachel of her beloved Dad. Everyone assumed, including Samuel's widow, that the business would be sold and there was certainly no lack of interest from potential buyers but Rachel was determined that her Father's legacy wouldn't be disposed of in that cavalier manner and vowed to take over the running of the business.

The news was met by a mixture of amusement and incredulity; how could a wee lassie possibly run a business like that? But they had all clearly underestimated the determination and business acumen of that particular "lassie" and the business didn't just survive but expanded even further. Even the loss of her Mother didn't dampen her drive and with Daisy there to look after the house and keep her fed and watered Rachel continued with renewed vigour.

It was in her fifty sixth year that she finally slowed down. Not that she wanted to but sadly her body started to refuse to let her work at the committed rate that had become her daily routine. Although she initially put it down to growing old she knew in her heart of hearts that it was more. A visit to the Doctor confirmed her worst fears and when, in that same unfortunate year, her sister Rebecca died, Rachel knew that the time had come.

The business was sold and Rachel left the Watson Milling Company office in Drumorty for the final time. She told all the staff members, who over the years had become more like friends than mere employees, that she would pop in from time to time to see them. Unfortunately that never came to past as within a matter of weeks she was bed bound.

Not everyone in Drumorty was fond of Rachel. There can be no doubt that on occasions she could have a barbed tongue, sharpened by years of dealing with farmers and merchants, many of who were only too ready to speak down to a slip of a girl, and as she grew older, any pretence at humouring people was totally forgotten. She also became somewhat bitter about the fact that her illness had robbed her of the chance to travel as she had always planned to do after she retired.

What upset her most, however, was her estrangement from her niece and nephew. It all arose from a minor family tiff with Rebecca about a family heirloom, their late Mother's Amethyst and Pearl brooch which was of very limited value but was much loved by both sisters. The dispute was successfully sorted out by the sisters over a meal with a few drinks and a trip down memory lane with Rebecca graciously allowing Rachel to keep it.

For some reason, however, Ronald or Amanda believed that their Mother had been slighted and refused to forgive their Aunt, shunning countless subsequent invites from Rachel to visit her. And when first Amanda and then Ronald married in the same year and didn't invite her to either event, Rachel was deeply hurt. Nevertheless she sent an expensive wedding present to both. Neither was acknowledged.

Despite all her contrariness I liked her and visited her regularly in her final days, Indeed I was by her bedside when Daisy entered to inform her that a Mister Ronald Wiseman and his wife were here to see her.

While waiting their arrival in her bedroom, Rachel, ever the cynic remarked, *"They're here before the coffin is closed and the will is opened."*

Ronald bounced in accompanied by a tall, skinny and angular young woman.

"Aunt Rachel. So good to see you again. It's been too long."

"Has it?"

"How are you keeping?"

"Do you normally enquire about the health of a skeleton?"

"So sorry you are not well. I don't think you've met my wife."

"No. I think my invitation to your wedding must have got lost in the post."

"Anyway, her she is. This is Miranda"

"Lovely to meet you at last Miss Watson."

"You don't sound like you come from Drumorty."

"Oh no I come from the South..."

"Stonehaven?"

"I was going to say the South of England. Winchester. Do you know it?"

"I know of it, if that's what you mean. Even country bumpkins like us have a little knowledge. But if you mean have I been there, then I haven't had that pleasure."

"It's very nice Aunt."

"I'll take your word for it. Must have been a bit of a hike for you Ronald seeing her home after a night out."

"No we met in Aberdeen. Miranda was at University there."

"So you're a student?"

"Was a student. I'm practising law now."

"Oh, and once you've practiced long enough do you think you will be any good at it?"

"I did warn you darling that my Aunt has an unusual sense of humour."

The icy and decidedly strained atmosphere in the room thawed slightly when Daisy shuffled into the room carrying a tray of tea things. I say shuffled as by then Daisy was also showing signs of advancing years, her knees swollen by years and years of crawling around scrubbing stone floors.

"Anyway Aunt Rachel we wanted to visit you and give you a bit of good news."

"*Good news? Please don't tell me Amanda intends visiting as well. I don't think I could stand the excitement.*"

"*Oh I rather suspect she will be popping in. But no, that's not the good news. Miranda's expecting.*"

"*Oh goody.*"

"*I knew you would be pleased. Miranda's parents are absolutely thrilled.*"

"*Yes Mummy and Daddy want to play a full part in helping to raise the child.*"

"*I thought they stayed in Winchester.*"

"*They do.*"

"*That'll be handy for babysitting.*"

"*Anyway, I better get to the real reason we are here today. We want to ask you something.*"

"*I think my purse is on the table over there.*"

"*No nothing like that. May we have your permission to call the baby Rachel if it's a girl?*"

"*You can call it that if it's a boy for all I care.*"

"*Great. Thanks a lot Miss Watson. Or should I call you Aunt*

Rachel?"

"No, Miss Watson is fine."

"Well we'll take our leave of you and let you rest. We hope to come back and see you again quite soon."

"Unless you would like to visit me in a wooden box, I would make that very soon."

They were barely out of her bedroom before Rachel spoke again. Just one word.

" Charlatans."

Whether Ronald and his new wife heard her or not is debatable. If they did it was the last word that they ever heard their Aunt Rachel say for less than a week later she was dead.

The next month a small group that included Ronald, his wife and his sister and her husband were gathered in the board room of the offices of Stephens and Hall, Advocates, for the reading of the last will and testament of Miss Rachel Watson, one which Mister Stephens explained had been *"altered slightly by Miss Watson only two days before she passed away.".* Several of those in attendance were on the edge of their seats wishing that the advocate would get beyond all the "sound mind" nonsense to the really important stuff. At last he did.

"I leave the sum of £500 to each of the employees of the Watson Milling Company listed below with sincere thanks for all their loyal service."

"To the unborn child of my nephew Ronald and his wife, whether it is called Rachel or not, I leave the sum of £10000 which will be held in Trust until his or her twenty first birthday in the hope that thereafter it is spent in a frivolous manner that his or her parents thoroughly disapprove of."

"To my nephew Ronald I leave the sum of £1000 and my father's old trouser press in the hope that he can at long last look dapper in his dress attire."

"To my niece Amanda I leave the sum of £1000 and the set of copper pans from the Rosebank House kitchen in hope that she can at last learn to cook."

"Rosebank House, all of its other contents and all other monies from my estate I leave to my dear friend, Mistress Jean Davie."

"That concludes the reading of the will."

For a matter of seconds you could have heard a pin drop before the room turned into uproar. Ronald, so red in the face that it looked like he was about to explode, was the first to speak.

"But...but..just who is this .....Jean Davie person."

A voice came from the rear of the room.

"That would be me."

Everyone turned in unison and stared at the woman who had just spoken.

The woman known simply as Daisy.

Drumorty Revisited

Drumorty 1931

I never heard from Bella again. For the first weeks or so I dreaded the knock on the door that would signal her return, back to collect her wee lad but as time passed I came to the conclusion that Bella was gone for good.

But the possible return of Bella wasn't my only fear. I was equally concerned that someone in Drumorty would stir up some mischief resulting in the boy being taken away to an orphanage and I decided that it would be sensible to consult my advocate.

Gerald Hall of Stephens and Hall had been the family lawyer for as long as I could remember, a good friend of my late father and a great help and comfort to me when Dad died and I was faced with sorting out his affairs.

There is little that goes on in Drumorty that remains a secret and news of the action I had taken quickly became the talk of the town with many publicly condemning the decision I had made.

Nae much wonder. Fit a waste of time and good money. I could hae telt her for naethin' that she would niver see hide nor hair of that lassie again. She had niver wanted that bairn in the first place and couldnae believe her good fortune when she found somebody daft enough to look after the wee boy while she flounced awa' trying to find the waster that had got her into that condition in the first place.

I almost felt sorry for Miss McLean. I mean it was bad enough that she was left haudin' the bairn, literally, but on tap of that thon Tocher quine niver returned the money that she stole. Mistress Bannerman telt Mistress Johnstone who confided in me that it was all of twenty three pounds that she ran awa' with. Imagine. Twenty three pounds. What a scoundrel.

It was two pounds.

The Librarian

I have always frequented Drumorty Library. A place of real serenity.

Silence is an essential element of library life and in Drumorty there was never any real problem in maintaining that sense of tranquillity for very few of the town's residents ever went to the place. On a good day, it would get a dozen visitors, on a bad one, Mister Brand, the librarian would open the doors at nine and close them at five, having barely seen a living soul in between.

Drumorty has never been a great seat of learning and so the library, which opened its doors amid huge excitement in 1910, courtesy of a charitable donation from the great Scottish philanthropist Andrew Carnegie, has seldom been thronged. But even the modest popularity it once enjoyed dwindled as Mister Brand became increasingly....forgetful.

For goodness sake woman, tell the truth. He went doo-lally and that's all there was aboot it. If you went looking for a certain book, which I very seldom did, he would tell you they were arranged on the shelves in alphabetical order. Only thing he couldnae tell you was which alphabet he had used; probably the Russian een by the look of it.

Blind eye aifter blind eye was turned afore things eventually came to a heid one day when the auld feel got so confused that he turned up at nine of clock at nicht to open up, sat on his own for hours and then locked up at five o' clock the following morning and went hame. Naebody would have been ony of the wiser if Jock Simpson, the milkman, oot on his morning delivery round, hidnae seen Mister Brand locking the library door.

The governors had to act and they pensioned him aff, presenting him with a gold watch for "services rendered". I aye thoucht that it was a bit of a daft thing to gie to somebody that didnae ken the difference a'tween nine am and nine pm. And so the library stayed closed for a few wiks while they searched for a suitable replacement. Personally I hoped that they would close the place for good and open a picture hoose, like the eens they had in Peterhead and Fraserburgh. It would certainly hae attracted mair folk but apparently the Carnegie crowd wouldnae agree. Spile sports.

You see I have niver seen ony point in books. I mean, fit interest dae I hae in made up folk bidin' in faraway places that I niver hae ony chance in seeing. I'm far mair interested in discovering fit real folk in Station Road or School Street, or even the folk richt next door, are up tae. And you canna read aboot that in books. You find can only find that oot by watching and listening.

But apparently Drumorty had to hae a library, even if few folk ever went intae it, and so a new librarian was employed. I couldnae believe it fan I heard the news. They had appointed an incomer. English! Aye English. Fan I was telt he was called Mister Charles Palmer I kent there would be trouble. And, as it turned oot, I was richt. But, of course, the first thing we had to find oot was whether or not Mister Charles Palmer was mairried.

Drumorty proved a most pleasant surprise to Mister Palmer. He had been warned that most of the population were inclined to give the library the cold shoulder but in fact on his first day he found them queuing up to join. Especially a large group of middle aged ladies who were so interested in the new librarian that at times he had difficulties in discharging his duties as he answered, or more often fended off, a barrage of questions about his private life.

"And fu are you the day?"

"Very well thank you Mistress MacKenty."

"And are you settlin' in a'right?

"*Yes as I said yesterday, I'm settling in very well.*"

"*I suppose this is a bittie different tae your last post?*"

"*No remarkably similar in fact.*"

"*And was that in a bigger place?*"

"*No. No, about the same size.*"

"*I see. Well we're delighted that you've chosen to come here Mister Palmer.*"

"*Thank you.*"

"*And is there a Mistress Palmer?*"

"*Oh yes. Several in fact.*"

"*Fit?!*"

"*Well there's my Mother and two of my brothers are married. Yes there are quite a few Mistress Palmers going about. Anyway are you wanting to borrow a book today Mistress MacKenty?*

"*Aye, I suppose I better. I'll tak' this een.*"

"*Judging by the layer of dust on it, it doesn't look like this has been a popular choice.*"

"*No it disnae that.*"

"'*Winter Notes On Summer Impression*'. I think he's a wonderful writer, don't you?"

"*Fa?*"

"*Dostoevsky.*"

"*Dost fa?*"

"*Fyodor Dostoevsky.*"

"*Oh him. Aye he's...rare.*"

"*You'll have read 'Crime and Punishment' I take it?*"

"*Dinna think so.*"

"*Oh you must. It's a classic. We may have a copy here. Would you like me to look?*"

"*No. It's a'right. I better see how I get on with this een first eh?*"

"*Probably. Mind you this isn't one of his more accessible works. But if you are an aficionado.*"

"*A fit?*"

"*A lover of his work.*"

"*Aye I suppose you could say that. Right, I better awa' hame and make a start tae it.*"

"Good idea. See you soon. No doubt."

Now it wasn't just the numbers that turned up daily at the library that surprised the new librarian but the regularity of their attendance. Clearly the ladies of Drumorty were very fast readers, returning weighty tomes within a couple of days of borrowing them. Of course, he rather quickly caught on to the fact that they were less interested in Little Nell or Robinson Crusoe than in a certain Mister Palmer and his matrimonial status, but as long as they were willing to frequent the library he was happy to string them along.

You see the Board of Governors, who had expressed doubts about the viability of a library in Drumorty, were delighted by the sudden upsurge of interest in the establishment. So pleased that they provided him with funds to enable him to expand the catalogue and he wasted no time in bringing in several rather formidable classics. Unfortunately some of his choices were not very well received in certain quarters.

Even goin' to the place ivery day, after a month neen of us were ony nearer to finding oot mair aboot oor new librarian. But Drumorty weemin' are doubty if naethin' else and we all valiantly stuck to oor task. It was a welcome relief when a supply of new books arrived as between us we had borrowed just aboot a'thing the library had to offer but little did we ken the kind of thing the new librarian was bringing into our midst.

I still mind that day like it was yesterday. I was standing in the street with a few ithers, just cleckin', when Mistress Nicholson came rushing in aboot, flushed and in an affa state. In fact it took us the best part of five minutes to quieten her doon sufficiently to get her to tell us fit was wrang.

It turned oot that she had borrowed een of the new books from the library, "The Interpretation of Dreams", and was frankly.... shocked. For once she had actually been interested in a book she had borrowed and had sat down the nicht afore to read it. And she just couldnae believe what she was reading; in fact at one stage she became so agitated that Henry, that's her man, had to ging next door to Mistress Broon's to borrow smelling salts.

She was still too distressed to tell us exactly fit the book was all aboot but from the brief description of its contents she was able to provide, it became crystal clear that a book like this had nae place in a God fearing, decent toun like Drumorty and that the new librarian should be suitably informed. And I kent just the person to put his bonnet on straicht for him.

"Good morning, Mistress MacKenty. Are you taking out this book

or returning it."

"Returning it. On behalf of a frien'."

"Oh yes, Mistress Nicholson borrowed it."

"A very upset frien'."

"Oh dear. And what seems to have upset her."

"I'll tell you fit upset her. This book. That's fit upset her."

"I'm sorry to hear that. I remember that when she found it amongst our new stock she seemed quite excited about it."

"Nae doobt. She thoucht it might help her with her problem."

"And what problem is that?"

"This recurring dream she's been haen for some time far she wins first prize at Drumorty Show for her cubbages."

"But why would a dream like that cause her distress."

"Because she disnae grow cubbages! Niver has. She thoucht that this book might help her to understand fit the dream was all aboot. Did it mean that she should give up with her rhubarb and start growing cubbages or fit?"

"I see."

"But, of course, there wisnae ony mention of cubbages. Just stuff about loons haen.....impure thouchts aboot their Mithers and filth like that."

"So you've read the book?

"I had tae. I mean I couldnae come in here and complain aboot it if I hidnae read it could I? That would hae been a bittie sma' minded would it nae?"

"I suppose so. This book is regarded as the definitive work on the subject of dreams."

"Nae in Drumorty it's nae.   Here it's regarded as filth. Fa is this mannie that wrote it onywiy?"

"Freud?"

"Aye him."

"Sigmund Freud is the world's leading psychologist."

"That's an affa funny sounding name. He disnae sound Scottish."

"No he's Austrian."

"Fit! You mean there are books by foreigners in Drumorty library?"

"Mistress MacKenty, you knew that already."

"*I certainly did not.*"

"*I hate to contradict you, but you did. You yourself borrowed a book by Dostoevsky.*"

"*Is he foreign?*"

"*Yes, he's Russian.*"

"*Russian! This just gets worse and worse. These books should hae a sticker on them "Written by a foreigner". Especially as now I see you're encouraging bairns to come in here.*"

"*Yes, I'm pleased to say that the children's section that we've opened has been very successful. Lots of them are coming in here after school every day.*"

"*And goin' hame with trash like this nae doobt.*"

"*No, they can only borrow children's books. They wouldn't be allowed to borrow the likes of Freud.*"

"*Nor should onybody else in Drumorty if you ask me. So if you wish to retain your regular customers then I suggest that you get the likes of this rubbish aff the shelves.*"

"*Perhaps we could confine it to reserve stock for a while.*"

"*And if you want anither bit of free advice, I suggest you are mair careful with your choice of new books in the future."*

"Yes. Thank you for that."

"Richt I've said my piece. I'm awa'."

"Don't you want to borrow anything?"

"No. I certainly dinna."

And he did take her advice to heart. After all he loved his job and was particularly thrilled by the success of the children's section. He was also wise enough not to underestimate the power of the vociferous Mistress MacKenty and her devoted followers. So he played safe, largely confining his acquisitions to reissues of tried and tested works by Dickens, Barrie, Bronte and the like until one day a new title caught his eye, "Doorways in Drumorty" by Lorna Moon, who he discovered was a highly successful Hollywood writer of screen plays.

He ordered a copy and was instantly enchanted by the author's beautifully captured vignettes of life in rural North East Scotland. She may have written the work in America but her short stories were remarkably true to life. He was so convinced that the residents of the town that had clearly inspired Miss Moon would love it, that he ordered another four copies and prominently displayed them in the entrance to the Library. It was not one of his better decisions.

"That's the final straaw."

"Oh, what's wrong now Mistress MacKenty?"

"You've just gone o'er far this time."

"I do wish you would explain to me exactly what I seem to have done wrong."

"Taken' in this Lorna Moon rubbish."

"I thought you would be impressed."

"Lorna Moon indeed! That's maybe fit she calls herself amongst her fancy friens in California but here we all ken fa she is. Nora Low, who's Mither used to rin a doon market Hotel in the High Street and whose Da used to sleep in a sheddie at the bottom of the gairden."

"Oh I see."

"It's certainly aboot time that you did. Aye, Nora Low who used to visit the bedrooms of male lodgers in the middle of the nicht and had to run awa' with a commercial traveller, een of your countrymen in fact, and get mairried in a hurry."

Drumorty Revisited

"I still don't understand why you are so upset."

"Because half of the population of Drumorty is in this book."

"Surely not."

"Surely aye! She may hae changed the names a bit but we recognise oorselves."

"Aren't you a little bit flattered to have been captured in print?"

"Flattered? Insulted mair like. Hiv you read some of the things she has said aboot us?"

"Yes I have read it. So you're suggesting that this Nora..."

"Nora Low."

"Yes that this Nora Low is telling lies about the local people."

"Now hing on a minute. I niver suggested that fit she'd written was untrue. Just insulting."

"Well, I'm afraid that we'll just have to agree to disagree on this particular subject."

"Oh will we? Laddie, if I've onything to dae with it you winna be here to agree or disagree with ony of us much langer. Your jaiket's on a shoogly peg already and it's just about to fa' doon."

I was horrified when I saw the photograph in the P. & J. of a group of the Drumorty ladies standing outside the Library, some holding up dreadful placards and others burning their library cards. I was also most disappointed to find that they were preventing anyone from entering the library, including the children who had loved to go there after school.

It took fully a month but eventually the Board of Governors bowed to the pressure and agreed to oor demands. All copies of THAT book were to be removed forthwith. All books broucht in by the new librarian were to be sent to ither libraries. If they wanted to turn their touns into modern day Sodoms and Gomorrahs that was up to them. The children's section was to be closed doon and Mister Palmer was dismissed. Aye, and withoot us finding oot onything else aboot him.

A few wiks later a new librarian was appointed. A local man.

Drumorty 1931

My advocate was wonderful. Not only did he convince the courts to leave the boy with me but succeeded in tracing Bella and getting her to sign adoption papers. Jamie was legally mine.

Of course that wasn't the name that Bella had given him. She called him Lawrence but what sort of name is that for a wee boy? So I decided to call him Jamie; it's a name that I have always been fond of.

By the time he reached the age of three, Jamie would spend his days watching the older children heading for and returning from Drumorty School, desperate to be like them. So I thought, why not?

We set up our own little "school" in a corner of the parlour with a lovely desk and chair which Robert Forrest made for us. I even managed to get an old blackboard the school no longer had any use for and we began daily lessons. Jamie just loved to learn and as a result by the time he turned five and enrolled at the School he could read and write and count. Now it may just sound like a proud Mum boasting but no, Jamie's teacher told me, in confidence obviously, that he was the star pupil of his age group.

I still remember with great affection that special day two months weeks ago when he dressed in grey shorts, a grey jumper, a white shirt and, of course, a Drumorty school tie. That was a proud day for us both as I walked him along to the school for the first time.

I will admit that I got some very strange looks on that first morning from a host of young lassies seeing their little ones off to school; I am sure a couple of the girls, who didn't know me, assumed that Jamie was being escorted by his grandmother but gradually they have grown used to the sight of me.

My favourite time of the day is three o'clock when I collect him and we walk home together, his warm wee hand in mine. He chatters incessantly about all that has happened that day and what all his new friends did and said.

Then when we get into the house he changes into his old clothes, without having to be told, fetches a glass of milk and a jammy piece and climbs onto my knee.

"Tell me a story Mum" he says.

Are there any more perfect words in the whole English language than those?

"Tell me a story. Mum"

Drumorty Revisited

Holiday & Help

This year you can enjoy a holiday that is just that bit different.

A chance to enjoy the pleasures of the beautiful Portuguese beach resort of Sesimbra together with the wonders of Lisbon and historic Sintra.

And at the same time, volunteer at the Bianca animal shelter which always has over 300 abandoned and neglected dogs and cats in its care.

You can spend as much or as little time as you want at the shelter helping in any way that you feel comfortable. Assisting with hands-on tasks, walking the dogs in the woodland areas near the shelter or simply spending time socialising some of the more timid of the creatures.

And we can make this dream holiday come true by assisting in a variety of ways, such as:

🐾 Providing advice on the easiest and cheapest flights to Lisbon.

🐾 Arranging transfers both ways between Lisbon Airport and your accommodation.

🐾 Booking accommodation at the beautiful but inexpensive Casa de Maria guest house.

We'll also assist on how best to enjoy the attractions of the area including information on travelling by bus to Sesimbra (15 minutes) and Lisbon (45 minutes). And much more.

For further information email biancaambassador@gmail.com or call 07903 463163.

www.bianca.pt/english